High Places

A PARABLE

by Rosemary L. Schwanke

Copyright © 2013 by Rosemary L. Schwanke
First Edition – May 2013

ISBN
978-1-77097-683-2 (Hardcover)
978-1-77097-684-9 (Paperback)
978-1-77097-685-6 (eBook)

All rights reserved.

This a fictious adventure story based upon fictious characters and events. Some places are fictious and other places are found in the world.

No part of this publication may be reproduced in any form, or by any means, electronic or mechanical, including photocopying, recording, or any information browsing, storage, or retrieval system, without permission in writing from the publisher.

Published by:

FriesenPress
Suite 300 – 852 Fort Street
Victoria, BC, Canada V8W 1H8

www.friesenpress.com

Distributed to the trade by The Ingram Book Company

Acknowledgments

Thank you to my supportive encouragers, especially Richard.

This story is not based upon any specific individuals, cultures or their belief systems.

Scriptural references are from the Authorized King James Version of The Holy Bible.

Chapter One
A Quest Begun
(I Have come For Thy Words)

Above the mountain peaks an eagle flies on the wind and its cry echoes down through the steep valleys like an eerie scream. It is pure and sharp. The air is cold and crisp and the sun is starting its climb up into the clouds above the dark mountains. Nothing seems to move. Nothing can be touched in this lonely, pure place. It is far from the grime and clamor of the cities. It is the place of rest and peace. How does a traveler get to this place? There is a path but who can find it?

Down below in the valley is a village. It is small and has only a few hundred inhabitants. Its people do not want many earthly things. They have lived this way for many years. Their homes are sturdy and cozy. They toil and they relax and toil again. The pace of life is slow. They do not want to go down further into the populous cities. Many of them only want to climb higher into the high country. They want to go up to what they believe is a pure place. It is known far and wide to be the place where one can attempt to climb a nearby mountain to reach a peaceful sphere. All seems well in the village but there is turmoil beneath the seemingly serene surface.

Further down, down and onto the lowlands are the hoards of busy inhabitants of industry and commerce. Everyone is in a hurry and everyone is anxious about their existence in the urban landscape that is crowded and confusing. New things and ideas multiply and then die and then rise again. The lowlands are tedious, ugly and competitive. It seems that little is known about the high country. They do not seem to look up.

In the city of Monsa lives a young, orphaned man who wants to know peace and truth. He is unlike his friends. He knows that there is something better. He works as a bellboy at a resort near the edge of his city. He gazes at the mountains in the distance and wonders. He has heard that there is a mountain that leads to a heavenly, peaceful place. He does not know that there are some who are looking for this mountain in the high country. Some do not know that they are looking for it. There is entertainment everywhere. Its noise seeks to blast out its messages to beguile any searching heart. The young man is tired of the noise of the city.

Ken is the young man from Monsa. He was tall with sandy, curly hair and blue eyes and when he smiled there was a hint of a dimple on his right cheek. He was always curious about many things and one weekend he decided to go to the mountains. On his way he stopped at the village in the valley. It was the Village of Wonder. He stopped at a small café for lunch. The owner was a big man named Will who laughed a lot. He told Ken that few people got to go to the high country. Many had tried but few had made it farther than a few hundred meters and then they ran back to the village. Ken was determined that he would succeed where others had failed. He gathered supplies and set off the very next day up a path that led up Black Mountain. There was a storm brewing but in his eagerness he didn't care. He was going to find truth and peace in the high country.

The rain pelted down on Ken but he climbed up, up and up. It grew dark and then he could not see at all. He stood still in the pouring rain and wished that he had brought a raincoat. He tried to set up a shelter but the wind blew it away. Ken was afraid. He sat on a fallen tree and shivered, realizing that he was not prepared for this environment. He was a city boy who knew nothing about camping in the wilderness. He decided that the next day he would return to the village and find someone who could guide him and teach him about survival in the wilderness. It was a long, cold and soggy night. The next morning Ken turned back towards the village.

The day was cloudy as Ken trudged toward the Bluebell Inn that he had stayed in that first night in Wonder. He was mulling over how he was going to get up the mountain. In the lobby he saw a man leaning against a wall staring at him. He came forward towards Ken and introduced himself as Ralph. Ralph was the local historian and before long the two of them were in deep conversation about the village and its history. Apparently this was an unusual little village. There were many different sections to the town. Each section had a different belief as to how to achieve happiness in the high country. Each section or group was distinctive in some particular aspect of interpretation as to how to get up into the high country. The only difficulty was that no one had ever successfully gone up Black Mountain. There were other mountains but no one had tried to climb any of them.

As Ken sipped his soup in the Sunrise Cafe, he thought about all these groups. Perhaps he should find out about them. He asked Will to tell him where to find a group. Will told him that these groups were quite rigid in their thinking and may not welcome him as he was an outsider. Ken was surprised to learn that Will had been asked to leave one group called the Green Group because he had objected to their dress code. They told him that he had to shave off his beard. Ken didn't have a beard and so he thought that he would find that group. Off he went down to the west side of the village. All the houses were green. That seemed strange to Ken. Every yard had one tree and a white fence around it. He knocked on the door of the first green house.

A large, friendly-looking lady with a big smile answered the door. Ken introduced himself and asked if he could be shown to the leader of the Green Group. Well, by chance this was the leader's home. A bearish-looking man came from the back of the house and stared at Ken with penetrating eyes. He asked why Ken wanted to talk with him and why he had come to their village. After Ken had explained his mission, the man introduced himself to Ken as Josh Brown. Josh told Ken that his group was the largest group in the village. Ken was welcome to attend a meeting that night in the Community Center. Mrs. Lucy Brown served some tea and cookies and then Ken went back to his hotel and slept until six o'clock. After a light supper at the Sunrise Cafe, Ken went to the Community Center.

Everyone there was wearing green. They were waving green flags and smiling a lot. Ken felt out of place. Everyone wanted to shake his hand. Word had got around that a new, possible member, was going to be at the meeting. Of course, they all knew that it was Ken. Everyone sat down and the hall was silent. Suddenly, a group of children came onto the stage singing a song about trees. Then everyone joined in and sang along with them with energetic enthusiasm. After that, Mr. Josh Brown came up to the stage and began to speak. Ken was astonished at what he heard.

With a thundering voice, Josh Brown declared that their cause was going to be on the winning side because they cared so much about God's creation. One day, very soon a plan would be announced as to how to go on The Great Trek. Everyone cheered loudly. Excitement filled the auditorium. Perhaps, this would be The Trek that would end with the promise of achieving entrance into the high country. Even Ken was getting interested. After that short speech, the Green Group divided into smaller groups to prepare for The Great Trek. Ken found himself in a group of young men his age. They were eager to make friends with Ken and he felt accepted right away. This group had to gather hiking equipment and divide it up so that each family had its share to use on The Trek. Ken felt that he could work with this group and so they all planned to meet again the next day.

The next day was sunny and bright and all looked well for a trip up the mountain. The word had to come to Mr. Brown that they would set forth up the mountain that very day at two o'clock. No one talked about the fact that they had never been successful in traveling more than a few hundred meters up the mountain path. That was a taboo subject. There was no discussion about past failures. Ken mulled this over but said nothing about it. He joined the young men and started distributing hiking supplies to every Green home. After that the Green Group met in the Community Hall for a rally of sorts with a scrumptious buffet afterwards to give everyone energy for The Great Trek. Songs were sung and everyone set forth in family and friendship groups. Josh Brown led the group with his family and other prominent families. There was not a cloud in the sky. As they neared the forest the Group formed a line on the well-worn path they had always taken. The people were quiet. Even the children behaved themselves. There was a strange quiet. Not even birds sang. Ken felt anxious.

Suddenly, a tremendous crack of lightening broke over them and everyone looked up at the suddenly darkened sky. Clouds had come from seemingly out of nowhere. Then the rain pelted down. Ken had never been in such a rainstorm. Water started climbing up to Ken's knees. Children began to cry as they were torn from their parents' arms and started floating away. The path had now become a raging river! This was a disaster! Ken and his group tried to help older people and children but some were swept along in the foaming, raging torrent. Josh Brown bellowed out that everyone should head back to the village. Somehow, after what seemed like an eternity, the Group sloshed, swam and floated their way back to the edge of the forest. Ken was astonished at what had occurred. The people were able to get back to their homes as darkness descended over the village. Ken wondered how many people had nearly perished or perhaps lost their lives over the years trying the get up that mountain.

Ken went to the Bluebell Inn and went up to his room. He was soaked and cold and hungry but most of all he was in shock. Was what had occurred a regular event? The Green Group seemed to ignore the dangers and kept trying to attain a goal that threatened to decimate their numbers. He began to question as to why he would attach himself to a group that flaunted with danger on a regular basis. Why did the people follow Mr. Brown? Did they think for themselves? Ken tossed and turned all night. In the morning he had a headache and he was congested. He slept for a while and then went to the Sunrise Cafe for something to eat. He was confused and depressed. He had also realized that if he was going to stay in Wonder he would have to obtain employment.

After eating a stack of pancakes, Ken started to read The Village Voice which was the only newspaper in the village. He had come to the realization that the Green Group was too strange for him. He was going to get a job that very day. In the ads at the back of the newspaper Ken read an ad for a gardener needed by some elderly people who lived in an apartment building called The Open Arms Apartments. Housing was offered on the property. This looked promising. He set forth for an address that took him to the western edge of the village, near the forest.

Ken approached a white apartment complex. He rang the bell at the entrance and an elderly, frail-looking lady with twinkling blue eyes and snow white hair came to the door. Ken introduced himself and told her that he had come about the gardener's job. She was delighted and she told him that Frank was going to come and talk to him about the job. She let him come into the lobby and led him to an apartment at the end of the hall. She knocked on the door and a very thin, small man with a large head and friendly face greeted them. Ken was ushered into the apartment and the lady left after saying farewell to Ken. Frank showed Ken a sitting room filled with big, soft sofas. There were bookcases on two walls. The room was cozy and looked out onto a lovely garden which could be seen through tall French doors. Frank offered Ken some tea and cookies.

The two chatted about the building and the property around it. Apparently, this apartment building housed mainly elderly people. They had lived there for many years in happy accord. The need for a gardener was quite desperate as the last gardener had died about two weeks ago. None of the residents were able to do this work and hence the ad had been placed in the newspaper. At the edge of the garden was a small, furnished house. Ken said that he was interested in the job. Frank told him that the job was his and that he could move in that very day! Ken was delighted! He already felt at home there. He didn't know why but after the events of yesterday and the frenzy of the Green Group, Ken felt that he was free and would now be able to start a new life for himself.

After getting his few belongings from the Inn, Ken went to the little house in the garden. It was perfect! It had a kitchen, sitting room, two bedrooms, a storeroom and a bathroom. That was all he needed. There was a shed with tools in it behind the house. Roses crawled all over the house. The aroma of the roses filled his senses as he lay down on his new bed that night. He slept soundly until the break of the next day. He awoke refreshed and ready to work. However, he had not filled the cupboards with food and so he set forth to spend his last few dollars on groceries at the only grocery store in the village. He went to The Food Basket to shop.

While picking up a can of corn, Ken was approached by one of the young men from the Green Group. Ken wanted to run but he smiled in a friendly manner. The young man, whose name was Ted, asked him if he wanted to come to a meeting that evening. Ken declined and muttered that he had a job now and that he couldn't attend meetings. That didn't seem to deter Ted at all and he told Ken that there would be another meeting on Saturday night. Ken decided to be straight with Ted and he informed him that he wasn't going to come to the Green Group meetings. Ted looked astonished. He asked Ken about his job and Ken told him for whom he was working. Ted's eyes grew wide and he looked hard at Ken. He told Ken that he shouldn't work for those people. Ken asked why but Ted said nothing more and turned on his heel and left Ken staring after him. Ken wondered why he would object to some old, harmless people. Ken was beginning to wonder if everyone got along in this village.

After he had made a breakfast of sorts for himself, Ken started weeding flower beds and digging in the large vegetable garden. This was the life for him! He had his own place. No one bothered him. The people of the apartment that he had met were really friendly. Frank came out later in the morning and told him about what needed to done and then invited him to his apartment for some coffee. Ken really enjoyed talking to the old man and wondered about what Ted had said about the people in this apartment. Ken really felt that Frank really listened and was interested in him. Frank told Ken that the people of the building met in the common room on the first floor every Sunday morning for a special meeting. Ken wondered if this was another Group trying to get up the mountain. He wasn't sure if he was ready to join the activities of another group after his experience with the Green Group. Ken went back to his work and the day passed pleasantly. Ken was very happy in his new situation. One of the ladies said that she had a kitten to give away and Ken thought that he would take it and make a pet of it. That evening Ken received his little bundle of fluff. It was a female short-haired kitten, orange, black and white. It was very vocal and bright. Ken decided to name her Echo. Echo and Ken were a little family in the little house at the edge of the forest below Black Mountain.

The summer passed all too quickly. The garden grew wonderful vegetables which belonged to various people in the apartment. Each person had his or her own plot. Even Ken had his own section. Ken had become acquainted with everyone in the building and they all were pleasant, friendly and nice to him. Echo had grown so fast. She was a bundle of energy. She went on her own private expeditions around the property but she always came back to the little house to be fed and to sleep at the end of Ken's bed every night. Ken had only met some of the Green Group people at various locations in the village as he went about his business. They were friendly but Ken got the feeling that they felt let down by his leaving the Group. Apparently, there was going to be another Trek in the Fall before the snow fell....

Ken had not joined in the Sunday meetings. He still felt uneasy about attaching himself to the group. He sometimes heard great singing on Sunday mornings. Toward the end of the summer Ken heard about yet another Group. The postmistress, who passed on gossip free of charge, told Ken all about this group. This group was in the center of the village. All of the houses in which the members lived were brown. They called themselves the Brown Group. They talked about caring for the Earth in order to find truth. They thought that if they were careful with the environment, they would be able to somehow find a way, safely, up the mountain. They too, had been unsuccessful thus far. Ken, felt that by now he was a gardener. He thought that he could get some gardening tips from these people but he didn't want to join the group.

A chance to learn more about gardening came one day when Ken read a poster at The Food Basket. The Brown Group was putting on a lecture about mulching. Ken decided that he'd go and see if he could learn something new. The next evening, in the Community Center, found Ken sitting in the audience of a group of people all dressed in brown. They looked like an army. The speaker was a lady with a flowery hat who spoke knowingly about her subject. Ken learned some new things about mulching and he was glad that he had come to the meeting. As he was leaving the Community Center the lady speaker asked Ken if he knew about the Annual Earth Picnic that was going to be held on the upcoming Saturday. Ken told her that he might come to it.

That last Saturday in August was a hot but humid day. A last blast of summer was the treat that day held for all who ventured out into the great outdoors. The Earth Picnic was held in a local park at the west side of the village. It was attended by not only the Brown Group but village members and others who appeared to be - Groups. Ken saw people dressed in red, brown, green, yellow, purple, pink and orange. Only a few were dressed "normally". What kind of village was this? Ken hadn't realized that there were so many groups in the village.

There were games, contests, prizes and lots of food. Ken had fun entering into some of the contests and he won some prizes. One prize was a huge pumpkin. He was eating some potato salad and a ham sandwich at a table with some of the people who were dressed in red. They told him that they were called The Red Group. Their philosophy was that this present life is the only reality and that if they concentrated hard enough, they would be propelled to the high country by their positive energy. Ken was astounded! They were a very serious lot. They didn't smile very much. One little boy commented loudly that Ken was eating meat. Many frowns appeared on the faces around the boy. Ken surmised that meat wasn't what they chose to eat on a regular basis. Ken thought to himself that here was yet another strange group. These groups didn't always wear their colors in public and so they weren't easily recognized. It was a strange feeling not to belong to one particular group in this setting.

As Ken wandered around he was glad to see Frank there with some of the people from the Open Arms Apartments. At last he'd feel more comfortable. They all smiled broadly as Ken approached them. They were munching on hot dogs and laughing about something. Edna, had just won a prize for her apple pie. The apples had come from the apple tree in the garden. Ken was pleased. They all rejoiced together and then they decided right then and there to eat it together! As they munched on the delicious pie at a picnic table, Ken noticed out of the corner of his eye that the groups were moving together and talking about something. They were all looking at the Open Arms group. Some were pointing at them. The happy little group didn't seem to notice or care but Ken was beginning to feel very uncomfortable. Before long the park was empty and only the little group at the table remained. Ken wanted to know why they had been pointedly left alone. Frank said it was because they were "old-timers" who didn't go along with the thinking of the various groups. Frank had seen groups flourish and die and then more groups spring up over the many years that he had lived in the village. The Open Arms Apartments was ostracized by the rest of the village. Ken couldn't think of the reason as to why they were not accepted. It hurt him to think that such great people were beneath the consideration of the other village members.

The Fall season was just ending and winter would soon be upon them. Ken wondered what to do for the dark, cold months. That problem was solved when he was given another job as caretaker which also included some general maintenance of the building. He got to go into the suites of some of the people. He had come to know some of them quite well. There was: Edna, who baked delicious treats for him, Ron who was a retired farmer, Betty who used to be a nurse and who offered various remedies for minor ailments, Tom who used to be a guide in a National Park, Jim and John (the twins) who used to work at a sawmill, Betty who loved needlepoint and who had given Ken some lovely pillows and then there was Jerry who used to teach at the local school. All these people were Ken's family, now.

One morning in late November there was a knock on Ken's door. Echo meowed loudly to get Ken's attention as he was just waking up from a deep sleep. Echo was staring at the door with her ears pointed forward. Ken wondered who would be at his door at seven in the morning. He threw open the door to find a stranger. A man was standing there and he looked lost. He indeed was lost and wanted to know how to get to Avona which was the nearest village. Ken had gone there once to buy some trees from a nursery. He had used Frank's old truck and it had been an uneventful trip. The village wasn't very impressive. The man looked frozen and Ken invited him into his humble abode to warm up by the fire. He gave him some hot tea and a biscuit. The man was very grateful and he was hungry. Ken made some scrambled eggs for him. His clothes were tattered and he looked unwell. He coughed several times. Ken asked him where he had traveled from that day and he replied that he had traveled from Torny which was a small town about fifty miles away to the east. As he was speaking, the man whose name was Jim White, suddenly fell off the chair he had been sitting on and lay there on the floor with his eyes closed. Ken was in a panic. He called up the Sunnyside Hospital which was the village hospital and soon the one and only ambulance appeared. Jim was taken away at once. Ken went along in the ambulance.

After Jim had been examined, Doctor Smyth told Ken that the man was completely exhausted and that he needed rest. They had taken some tests and the results would come in a few days. The hospital would keep him under observation for a while. Ken said that he would pay the hospital bill. Ken felt that Jim would not have any insurance or money to cover the costs. Ken felt very sorry for this man who looked as if he was alone in the world. Jim was probably in his late fifties. Ken wondered about his family and where they lived.

The Open Arms residents adopted the stranger in their midst. Some came to hospital to chat with him. He had awakened from his collapse and was sitting up in his bed. Some brought flowers and fruit. He was looking better every day and soon he was well enough to leave the hospital. Jim had disclosed to Edna, one day when she was visiting him in the hospital, that he really didn't have a home and that he was trying to relocate to a small town or village and that this village seemed to fit the bill. He was a retired miner and he had worked for many years at a mine near the city of Zim. The coal dust had affected his lungs and he had retired a few months ago. He had never married and therefore he was free to find another place of residence. He had a modest pension.

The Open Arms residents decided, at a hastily called meeting, chaired by Frank, that they would all chip in to pay the rent on an apartment (which had recently been vacated due to the death of the tenant) for Jim. Jim was overjoyed to hear this news. The residents busied themselves to find furniture and home furnishings to make Jim's new home cozy and welcoming. There was much excitement in the air as Ken drove Frank's truck into the driveway of the Open Arms Apartments. Jim was sitting next to him. They were all standing at the front door with broad smiles on their happy faces. Jim was trying to fight back tears that were threatening to trickle down his cheeks. He thanked them all for their concern and great generosity. They all laughed and ushered him into his apartment which was on the first floor. Frank pointed out to Jim that they would be neighbors. After showing Jim his accommodations, which he definitely approved of, the cheerful throng gathered in the common room to enjoy some refreshments provided by Edna and some of her fellow bakers. Ken was glad that all had worked out so well for Jim. The kindness of these people always amazed him.

On the last day of November the Green Group had planned their last trek for the year. They had made sure that they were fully prepared and that they were ready for anything, so said Ted as he chatted with Ken on the main street one Saturday morning. Ken wondered what possessed these people to go on these useless hikes. They flirted with danger. The weather was getting more unpredictable every day and soon it would snow. What would happen this time? Surely these people would decide against going once again up that mountain.

The day for the trek dawned clear and bright but it was somewhat chilly. Ken watched the group assemble at the edge of town and start on their way. Green flags were waving and loud cheers ascended into the crisp air. Soon they were out of sight. Ken kept watching to see what would transpire. Frank had told him that several times the Green Group had had to be rescued by the villagers. It started to snow and then a wind whipped the hat off Ken's head. This did not seem to be a good omen for the fate of the trekkers. Soon Ken was standing in the midst of a snowstorm. Now he was really worried. He stumbled several times as he fought his way towards the Police Station. He told them that a rescue party would be needed for the Green Group. They had helped those people several times and so they quickly organized a search party and set off at once to find this group and bring them back safely.

About an hour later the rescue team successfully brought every group member back to safety. They had been rescued just in time. Some of them had just about fallen over a steep cliff and they were all quickly becoming disoriented as the snow swirled around them. They were rejoicing, though, that they had got further up the mountain this time. That was all they chatted about as they sat in blankets and sipped hot chocolate in the Community Center. Ken was totally amazed. Any suggestions about their not ever going up the mountain again would have been met with great derision. Ken bit his lip and said nothing. They were singing that tree song again! He had had it with these people! Soon, Ken would find that there were even stranger people in this village.

Christmas holidays were fun for Ken because he spent most evenings in the apartments with his friends. They spoiled him royally. Frank and Jim had become fast friends. Jim even went to the Sunday meetings. Ken still didn't want to go to any type of group meeting. Frank often referred to a Book that he used in the meetings. Ken thought that a Book was probably better than songs about trees. Still, Ken didn't want to be totally identified with them. He wasn't sure why he felt that way but, there it was and he couldn't shake his feelings about it. Frank joked that one day he'd come and join them.

The Red Group was the next group to stage an attempt up the mountain. They had a unique way of "setting out". They all formed a circle and hummed. This humming went on for an hour. Other villagers watched this performance. It was entertainment. There was an expectancy in the air as the humming stopped and silence descended upon the group and those who watched, Ken included, waited to see what would occur. The group stood with bowed heads and said nothing for another hour. Ken's feet were freezing. He'd had enough of this craziness and he started to leave but someone in the watching audience motioned him to stay as if something would soon transpire.

Suddenly the group raised their heads and shouted a strange word. They shouted it louder and louder. Ken covered his ears. He had to get away from these people! Just as he was about to move, a voice from the group yelled that someone in the audience was affecting their ceremony. The audience was told not to move. Ken was outraged. He'd move if he wanted to and no one was going to stop him! A lady next to him nudged him and gestured with her hands that he should stand still. Ken thought better about moving and decided to wait and see what would transpire.

The audience stood frozen in silence. A scruffy looking man emerged from the group and started towards the audience. He slowly advanced toward the watching, wondering crowd. He started to look deeply into the eyes of everyone in the front row. No one moved an inch. The man muttered that he'd find the source of negativity if it took him all day. Ken had had more than enough. He carefully tried to edge his way out of the audience. The man saw him move and came toward him like a stealthy panther. Ken started to run and he didn't stop until he had reached his house. The man had given up chasing him and had returned to monitor the negativity. Ken ran to his bedroom and lay down on his bed and stared at the ceiling. This village was getting to him. He had come to find peace and all that he had found were groups of mad people running around doing the strangest of things all in the name of trying to find the truth. He didn't even want to know if they got up the mountain or even to the bottom of it. The only bright sparks in this dark place were the dear people of the Open Arms Apartments.

The next day was sunny and cold. Ken decided to take a walk in the forest near his little house. It was a Saturday and so he had the time to do some exploring. He was warmly dressed and he'd planned to be out for only an hour. He enjoyed breathing in the clear air. He saw some white rabbits hopping in the snowdrifts. Crows called and scolded. Ken was feeling more himself today. He was following a path that went horizontally around the edge of Black Mountain. He heard a rustling in the trees ahead and he thought it was a deer. Then he caught a flash of yellow. As he got closer he saw more yellow. As he turned a corner in the pathway he saw a campsite of sorts composed of yellow tents. People were sitting around a campfire laughing loudly. They all wore yellow. Ken's mood changed. Another group on a camping trip was all he needed! However, his curiosity got the better of him and he stopped walking and hid behind a huge tree.

This group was indeed a jolly bunch of souls. They were roasting marshmallows and singing what seemed to be campfire songs. A tall, thin man stood up and started to talk and as he launched into his story, various people laughed loudly. Ken thought that they were rude by interrupting this speaker but the speaker smiled broadly and seemed to encourage this gaiety. Ken crept closer and as he moved he stepped on a dead twig and it snapped loudly. Everyone turned and looked right at him! He feebly smiled and they motioned for him to join them around the fire.

Ken was given a roasting stick and joined right into eating marshmallows. He hadn't eaten much that day and so he roasted more than a few over the crackling, red hot fire. People around the fire introduced themselves and the tall, thin man said that he was Brother Joyous. The ladies were called Sisters and the men were called Brothers. Ken wondered about that but didn't inquire about it. This was yet another group with their own peculiar quirks. The names of the people were strange, too. Some of their names were: Sister Merry Merry, Brother Happy, Sister Laughter and Brother Mirth. Brother Joyous decided that it was time to sing and so all, except Ken, joined in and sang a loud rendition of what probably was their theme song. The words were: "Happy, happy, we are happy. All we want to do is laugh and enjoy. All we want is to live life with a contented, joyous heart." They sang it about ten times. Each time they were louder and some got up and clapped and swayed with the beat. At the end of it (finally) they all collapsed into spasms of yelps. Ken was astounded. He was also very uncomfortable. These people had worked themselves up into some kind of altered state. He wanted to get out of this forest and into his little house and lock the door! However, that was not possible. He was jammed between two jolly, very enormous men. The people around the fire kept on laughing. Some were rolling around in the snow at the edge of the campfire.

Finally, after about fifteen minutes of this behavior, Brother Joyous, (who had wiped the snow off his pants, as he was one of those who had done the 'snow roll') got up and proclaimed that their Joy Time was over and the next "event" was for everyone to go into their tents for meditation. Ken was frightened. He looked for a way out and he saw it when the two men stretched and started towards the tents. Many of the group asked Ken to join them but he said that he had to get back and feed his cat and do his chores. Thankfully they accepted this explanation but insisted that he come tomorrow to join in their athletic contests which would help them gain strength for the mountain trip. Yes, they planned to ascend the heights of Black Mountain. Ken waved good-bye and hurried as fast as he could without breaking into a run. He had to get out of there!

He was so glad to get back to his house and to his cat. Echo meowed and rubbed against his legs, signaling that it was time she was fed! He was still somewhat shaken by the events of the day. As Echo nibbled her food in her pink dish near the window, Ken slowly sipped coffee and ate a doughnut which had been baked by Edna. He pondered for a long while on all of the groups in this village. Each group had a way to get up the mountain but not one of them had made it up there. Why did they keep on trying when they were obviously failing? As the sun set in the west, Ken decided that he was so tired that he'd turn in early. He lay in his bed and stared at the ceiling. Perhaps he should return to Monsa. He hadn't met strange groups there but he didn't have any family there because he was an orphan. He came to the realization that his family was the Open Arms residents. He concluded that he had no reason to return to the city. After all he was on a quest for peace and truth and he hadn't found it there. He was confused, upset and unhappy in his inner most self. What was the meaning of life? Where was it all leading to? The mountain was supposed to be the source of truth. Everyone in the groups believed that but why was it so difficult to get there? Perhaps he'd talk to Frank about all of his questions. He finally fell into a fitful sleep in which fires raged and people's faces leered at him with big toothy smiles and insane laughter was heard in the background.

Chapter Two
A War of Sorts

The next day Ken went to talk to Frank about all the questions in his mind and heart. Frank was puttering around in his study, dusting his bookshelves. He was glad to see Ken as he hadn't spoken to him for a while. He had just returned from a trip to visit his children in Semile, a city to the north. Everyone was fine, he told Ken. He had two new grandchildren which had nearly worn him out. He was enjoying peace and quiet again. Frank put on the kettle to boil for tea. He had a special tea made with dried herbs from the garden. Ken really liked to drink it. Ken enjoyed discovering all the interests that this man had and the wisdom he had accumulated over the years.

Frank poured the tea from his favorite blue teapot (which he had made) into Ken's blue mug (also made by Frank). Frank presented Ken with an assortment of cookies and small cakes. Of course, they had been baked by Edna. As Ken munched on a sugar cookie he began to launch into his questions. Frank listened respectfully, nodding now and again and encouraging him to continue when Ken hesitated. Finally all of his questions and frustrations had been laid out and Ken fell silent. Frank said that these groups would cause one to question his or her sanity. Over the years all had not been peaceful between the groups. Frank disclosed that he had heard some rumors about a duel that was going to be fought soon. Ken was shocked. He almost dropped his mug of tea. He didn't know that duels were still fought. He asked what kind of duels were fought. Frank explained that it was a duel of words and ideas or philosophies. There was a judge and jury and they decided who had won the duel. The losers had to leave the town! Ken was amazed. He asked Frank how many groups had left and he told Ken that many had left but there were always new groups coming into the village as it was the nearest village to Black Mountain.

Ken had never really asked Frank why he and the others in the Open Arms Apartments had never tried to get up the mountain. Frank told Ken that the mountain wasn't special. It was not the way to peace and truth. Ken stared at Frank. Was he mad? It was common knowledge that climbing up Black Mountain was the only way to true fulfillment. Frank shook his head and said that it was not the way. Ken didn't want to stay any longer. He made some sort of excuse and left quickly. No one had the answers! Now there was going to be a stupid duel! He had a massive headache. He went to the grocery store to get a bottle of aspirins for it. On the bulletin board he saw a poster proclaiming a duel set for next Friday in the Community Center. It was going to be at seven o'clock. The Red Group and the Orange Group would debate the topic: 'Is There Another Mountain We Should Climb?' Ken hadn't run into the Orange group yet. He could hardly wait to find out what they believed. He didn't have long to wait. Right there in the store he saw two of them by the till. Ken hailed the two young men as they proceeded to leave the store. He told them that he'd pay for his aspirins and then he wanted to talk to them. They smiled and said that they'd wait for him outside.

Outside the store the three young men fell into earnest conversation. Ken found out that duels were engaged in quite regularly. A group had to duel another group every month or so because the tally was taken at the end of each month. Ken asked what the tally was and they told him that it was a counting up of the number of attempts up the mountain that month. The more attempts the worse off it was for a group because as everyone knew: no group had EVER got up the mountain. The greater the number of attempts meant the more chance of failure for a group. The Oranges and the Reds were up against it because they both had tried ten times in the last month! Ken was astonished that all this had been going on and he hadn't witnessed much of it. He asked the young men, who were curiously called by the names: Pine and Apple, if there was a place to find information as to when groups would be trying to ascend the mountain. They looked at each other and laughed. They told him that there was a notice board in the Community Center on the back wall. All kinds of information about groups and their activities was put up on it for all to read.

Ken asked Pine and Apple what their group believed and when he heard it he almost fainted. They believed that by eating a diet of citrus fruit and by having good self concepts they'd ascend to the heights. Unfortunately some members had to be regularly expelled from the group because they didn't follow the diet and some fell into self doubt and despondency because they lost hope in the group vision or … group think. Their group had been depleted down to about fifteen members. Ken knew that he'd never survive in such a group! The twins invited him to come to a meeting but Ken declined. He enjoyed his meat too much and he was often filled with self doubt and anxiety. He said that he'd come to the duel. They departed amiably and Ken headed to the Community Center to check out the bulletin board.

Ken pushed open the door and went into the Community Center. There was a group at the front standing around in purple shirts. They were talking earnestly about something. Ken walked as closely as he could without trying to get their attention. A small woman in a long purple dress with a matching wide, purple hat was almost yelling in her high pitched voice. Not everyone was listening to her as many of them wanted to talk at the same time. Finally, a middle-aged man shouted for them to stop and they did just that. He launched forth in a tirade against the group saying that they had forgotten their own principles and that if this continued they'd be finished as a group. Everyone was now completely silent. He told the group (which numbered about thirty) that they all needed to leave and then they could come back later on that night to resume their plans for the next Mountain Attack. That's what they termed their treks up the mountain. It was an attack. Ken hid under a bench until they all had shuffled out in their purple-hued costumes. Ken wasn't impressed with this group!

As Ken neared the bulletin board he heard a tiny sound. He turned around but no one was there and so he proceeded to look at the information before him. There was so much going on in this village! Every day the groups met and sometimes they tried to go up the mountain. The failures of each group were carefully documented. The least number of tries had been made by the Pink Group. Their philosophy was different from the rest in that they believed that all the groups should unite into one powerful group. They spent much of their time trying to engage other groups to join with them and with other groups but it did not appear that they had had much success. Each group was fiercely independent. The Pink Group spent a lot of time in planning social events to lure others to join. They also were known for many worthwhile community assistance programs. They had only made one attempt on the mountain. All the belief systems of the groups could be read and compared on this bulletin board. Ken saw a pattern. All had colors, all had never made it up the mountain, all thought that what they believed was the truth and all were separate from the other groups. The bottom line, thought Ken, was that they were all failures and they were wasting their time. Maybe he'd form a group of one or two or.... He mused about what his own belief system was and he found that he really didn't have much to offer himself or others. What a pickle! There were the Open Arms people who didn't care about the mountain and then there were the groups who really cared but who were failures and then there was himself who cared but didn't have a clue about how to make it up there.

After leaving the Community Center Ken stood looking up at the looming peak of Black Mountain. It was only a mile up and it would not take long to get up there. Maybe these people weren't going on the right path. He thought that in the near future he'd explore around the base of the mountain and try to find a good starting off point. It was getting dark and starting to snow. Ken hurried back to his house and lit a fire in the fireplace. He sat in his comfy chair with Echo on his lap. Ken was feeling more independent by the minute. He'd find his OWN way! These people were losers but they were sure entertaining! The war in his mind was quelled. He didn't need anyone to show him the way.

The night of the duel arrived. Ken did not want to miss it. He was at the Community Center about half an hour early. Two tables were being set up on the stage. There were four chairs at each table. The two groups were clustered together separately discussing what appeared to be serious concerns. Ken was going to enjoy this debate. He relaxed in his chair in the second row. He had a good vantage point as he was right near the center aisle. The tables were draped in the group colors of orange and red. Each group had its own banner on a stand beside their table. There were some more chairs a little farther apart from each table for other team members to sit in and to cheer or boo or whatever they did at a duel. Ken didn't know what just exactly the order of events would be but he didn't have to wait long as someone passed him a printed copy of what would occur that night. It looked quite complicated. As Ken read the paper, people started to fill up all available seats. Soon the hall was completely filled and a buzz of anticipation filled the air.

None of the Open Arms people were there and Ken wasn't too surprised as they didn't seem to be interested in other groups' meetings. An elderly man sat next to Ken. He introduced himself to Ken and told him that his name was Bryn White and that he had lived in the village all of his life. He told Ken that he had been at many duels and they were always interesting. Soon the duel was called to order by the lady in the long purple dress. She told everyone that the audience was not to say a word. Only group members could comment or cheer on their fellow members. Ken remembered reading about the purple group. Apparently, since it was the longest standing group existing in the village, it had the right to chair meetings between groups as well as duels. They stood for order and law. Ken didn't think that they would survive much longer as a group because of what he had witnessed a few days before in that very spot where Lily Royale (the chairperson in the purple dress) now commanded attention from the large crowd.

The audience was hushed and silent. The Red and Orange members filed to their tables. Ten members on each side sat in their chairs away from the tables but they were still on the stage. Lily Royale gave some guidelines to each group about not interrupting and only speaking for three minutes and then she read out the duel topic which was whether there was another mountain they should climb. The leaders tossed a coin and the Red group leader won and he made an opening statement. He was going to show everyone that Black Mountain was the only mountain to climb. He had proof. The Orange group leader then told everyone that Black Mountain was finished and that he'd discovered another nearby mountain that looked very promising. He'd lay out the real truth about Black Mountain. Each side cheered their leader loudly.

The four members of the Red group took turns at explaining that Black Mountain was The Way. There had always only been one mountain to climb. Everyone knew that because of ancient writings that a long ago disbanded group had kept. The Red group leader claimed that he had access to these writings but he could not reveal them because they were very fragile and could not be disturbed. The Orange group booed long and loudly at this revelation. They wanted tangible proof. The Orange leader demanded real evidence that all could see and touch. The Orange group yelled out, "YES!"

Back and forth the two groups verbally sparred. The Orange group hinted that their new mountain was an easy climb. However, they had not climbed it. There were more boos. A tally was being taken by Lily Royale and she called half time and revealed that the Orange group was ahead by one point. Everyone stood up and stretched and helped themselves to refreshments at the back of the hall. Ken saw many different group members that he recognized in crowd. They all stood together looking at members from other groups. The dueling groups were huddled at the front like football teams at half time. Ken hailed his old acquaintances from the Green group. They were polite but somewhat distant. There was some tension in the air and Ken wondered why as this was only a debate.

When he got back to his seat, Bryn told him that now the fireworks would begin. Ken wondered about this observation. Bryn should know, thought Ken. The second round was heated and loud. Each group was floundering around in suppositions and half-truths. Then the name calling began. Lily Royale reminded them of the rules. No interruptions and no disrespect was going to be tolerated any longer. When one member of the Orange group called a member of the Red group, "a big, fat pig", chaos erupted. Lily called a stop to the duel. The duel would have to be resumed the next evening to allow for a cooling down period. There was one more round to go and it would have to wait for the next day. Ken asked Bryn if this was the usual order of events. He told Ken that once in a while this occurred. However, it was not the usual order of events. The Orange group had lost their point due to the name calling and so the two groups were now tied. Everyone in the audience was muttering and shaking fingers and heads at the groups on the stage. The dueling groups were strangely silent.

Ken could hardly wait for the next evening to come and he kept himself busy the next day doing some maintenance chores in the apartments. Frank was friendly and asked Ken about the duel. Ken told him that it was going to conclude that evening. Frank said that he was glad that there had been no violence. Was he hinting that there had been violence in the past? Ken was afraid of the answer. He didn't talk about the duel anymore. Secretly he wondered about The Book Frank had referred to at one time and he wondered if it was like the ancient documents that the Red group claimed they had in their possession. He helped Jim move a table into his apartment. Jim had found a bargain at a rummage sale held by the Pink group. Jim seemed so contented with his life. Ken was a little envious.

The big night came and again Ken was early and right there in the front of the auditorium. Everything was set up again as it was the previous evening. The two groups were talking quietly and calmly. Ken thought that there probably wouldn't be another blow-up. People quickly filled up the seats and Lily Royale stood up to reiterate the rules (which would be STRICTLY enforced). Ken noticed a young woman sitting in the front row ahead of him. She was dressed in purple. He wondered if she was Lily's daughter. She was smiling at Lily and Ken was not surprised to see Lily sit down beside her. The two groups started their duel. It was the last round and they had to summarize their positions.

In his summary statement The Red group leader held up some yellowed frayed papers and declared that these were copies of the ancient documents. These documents detailed a route to travel up Black Mountain. Although the Red Group had tried to find this route, they had not found it as yet. They believed that they were very close to discovering it and by mind projection they would literally float up the mountain. The audience laughed. The Orange Group burst out into explosions of mirth. They were a group founded upon reality (so they thought) and one could see the derision they held for the Red Group members.

Then it was time for the Orange Group leader to present his summary. Their new mountain, White Mountain was close by and would probably be easy to ascend. Why not try a new mountain as Black Mountain was a lost cause? Perhaps truth could be found there as it was so close to Black Mountain. He downplayed the ancient documents as being unimportant. This was a new era and a new focus had to be found. Repeated failure wasn't getting anyone anywhere. There was a silence one could cut with a knife after he sat down. It was clear that this was the winning argument.

After this, a vote was taken by the members of the Purple group. The Orange group had easily won the duel. The Red group would have to leave the village. They would have to leave that very night! The audience shouted, "Shame!" several times. The Red group silently filed out of the hall. The audience took up a chant. They chanted, "Go, Go, Be Gone and Come Back Not!" Ken could hardly believe his ears! What had happened here? The old order had been toppled. It had always been known that Black Mountain was The Mountain to climb. Now it seemed that there might be a new way to try and it was close to the village. He was very uncomfortable about the way the losers had been treated. It seemed to be a tradition that probably went back centuries. Lily and the young woman came up to Ken and he asked them what the groups would do now that Black Mountain had been discredited as a viable way to truth. Lily said that the groups would have to decide for themselves. She introduced the young woman as her daughter, Star. Star said that she was sad for the Red group. Ken thought she looked pretty and that she seemed to be very pleasant. She had blue eyes and red hair. He was suddenly shy and so he said goodbye to them and he left quickly.

Ken's head was in a whirl. This village could be quite cruel. All was not so serene below the surface. He was more determined than ever not to join a group. He didn't want to be publicly shamed and driven out of the village. He'd do his own searching without anyone's help. Now he could try the other mountain. No one would know what he was doing because he was a free agent. He would trust no one and be very careful in his explorations.

Chapter Three
Fresh Revelations

Slowly, the winter winds and snow turned to warmer winds and slush. The grass appeared, buds on trees and bushes gradually turned to leaves and the first hardy flowers appeared in the gardens. Ken loved this time of year and he was excited because he had great plans for the garden. A vision for his garden emerged in his mind as he put fresh soil on the flower beds and planted bulbs and seeds he had harvested from last summer. He had plans for a rose trellis. It would have pale pink and dark red roses intertwined on the trellis. "Gardener Ken" was glad that he had pruned back all of the plants in the fall and he had allowed the dead leaves to rot on the flower beds. The soil was rich and black. During the bitter winter months he had mused about his dream garden. Now he was able to start to work on creating a masterpiece.

Although he was busy outdoors, he had not forgotten his mountain quest. He had walked around the base of White Mountain and he thought that he had a way to climb it but it would take careful and stealthy planning. Many groups often camped in the woods near the base of the mountain. What they were doing, Ken did not know or really care. They seemed to be trying to get into the proper mood to assail the heights. Some groups were quite noisy. The Yellow group, of course was quite loud in its boisterous camp meetings. Their laughter could be heard for miles. Ken had to shut his window a few times because they disturbed him in the middle of the night. As the weather got warmer, more groups went camping and soon it seemed that half of the village was living among the trees. The Green group took up a large part of the forest but they complained that other groups were destroying the vegetation. The Brown group went around cleaning up the garbage left by careless campers. They thought that these good deeds to help the Earth would also give them favor in the quest to climb White Mountain. They had a very self righteous air about them.

They issued complaints on the bulletin board and named names from the groups who were the biggest offenders. A new group had come to town and it quickly got to work in building a commune of sorts at the western side of the village. They claimed to have a message for all the groups and they called themselves the Blue Group. In fact there was going to be a special meeting for all groups and any interested spectators where a revelation was going to be presented by this new group.

One day as Ken was deciding between two different kinds of pansy baskets in the Garden Patch (the village plant shop), Star appeared as if out of nowhere and said hello to him. She was buying some plants for her own garden and soon the two young people were talking about their garden plans. She said that she would like to see what Ken had done so far in his garden. They agreed to meet there the next day around ten in the morning. Ken thought she looked very nice with her red hair in a pony tail. He found it very easy to talk with her and he looked forward to seeing her again the next day.

The next day found Ken up early and ready to present his garden to his new friend. However, that day would turn out to be quite a disaster. As he was weeding his flower bed by his house he saw a flash of blue out of the corner of his eye. He turned around and suddenly, seemingly almost in an instant, a middle-aged couple, dressed in blue overalls, came towards him with a large net. Before he knew it, the net was over him! He fought to get out of it but these two were very strong! He could not budge the net as they were firmly planted on it with their feet. They informed him that he was the chosen human for their next day of Blue Magnificence! Ken had no idea what they were blubbering on about and he renewed his efforts to get out of the net. He also screamed at the top of his lungs. Frank and Jim came running and the two captors ran away like blue streaks into the forest. Ken was helped out of the net by the men and they all sat down on a garden bench to discuss what had just occurred. No one knew who the people were and the three of them were all shaken by this experience.

When Star appeared about twenty minutes later, Ken was still in a state of shock and he told her that they'd have to look at the garden another day. He told her what had happened and she was very upset. She told Ken that these new people had caused many problems. Star left soon after that and Ken rested for about an hour. He wondered if he should go to the police. However, he pushed that thought aside as they were always being pestered about various nefarious deeds of different group members and they probably would brush this incident off as a prank of sorts. In reality, the groups ruled the village. Ken was getting increasingly uneasy in this atmosphere. He had been painfully made aware that unstable characters were wandering around and some of them should be locked up!

The day of Blue Magnificence dawned a few days later. The Blue group had taken over the main street with a parade of blue wagons pulled by horses draped in blue. The group members wore feather headdresses and each one seemed to be blowing on a strangely shaped horn. The noise was horrendous. Ken warily watched from the back of the watching crowd. He didn't want to be noticed and captured. This group had come from a town five hundred miles away. Ken heard this from a man standing near him who was talking to a lady with a small baby. They mused that this group was probably thrown out of the town. The parade stopped and a thin man with a long white beard announced that he was Brother William and that he had a message for all that would cheer and energize their souls.

Brother William stood on a wagon surrounded by several rotund women with cherubic children. They all smiled adoringly at him as he spoke to the crowd. He held a blue scepter in his right hand. A long blue cloak flowed down to his black boots. In a surprisingly strong and commanding voice he blasted all who would doubt the sincerity of his group. They had chosen Wonder for their habitation because they cared for its inhabitants. They had been led to Wonder by the Great Bird who pointed them to the village. Many people in the audience laughed. Some jeered and some threw pebbles at the horses which caused them to become skittish. Brother William said that there were always doubters but soon they would believe if they gave the group a chance. Someone yelled out asking where the Great Bird was and Brother William replied that it had gone back to its home in the Blue Mists. More laughter rose from the crowd. Soon the crowd started yelling at the Blue Group to leave and go back to The Bird. Brother William calmly gathered his people together and the parade became a silent file of wagons heading down the street presumably to their commune. The day of Blue Magnificence had turned into a nightmare. Ken rushed away back to his little home.

The Blue Group was shunned by the villagers. They were "so far out" that they weren't allowed to use the Community Center. When the Blues shopped or did any business in the village, people gave them a wide berth. This was the strangest group to ever land in the village. The other groups all united in solidarity against them. Each group had its spies. The spies would sneak up on the group and gather information about their activities. They reported back to their groups. Soon all the groups planned to gather together for a meeting about what to do about these weird people in their midst. Ken had heard some of the strange reports and tidbits about this group. Star had come over to look at his garden and she told him that the Blue Group lived together in a large blue tent. It was like a circus tent. They kept warm with fires which burned day and night. There was widespread fear that there might be a fire. Their horses roamed everywhere and seemed to be ill-cared for as they were scrawny. Their "music" was heard at odd hours day and night and this kept many people from a good night's sleep. This group was a major irritant. The most galling aspect about this group was that they declared they were going to ascend White Mountain soon and be successful!

Chapter Four
The Blue Nightmare

One day a horse wandered into the Open Arms garden and started nibbling the grass. Ken tried to shoo it away but it just stared at him with sleepy brown eyes. When it started eating his flowers, Ken started to yell at it. From behind a tree Ken saw two blond children staring at him. They looked skinny and sickly. They were dressed in blue. Ken guessed that they were from the Blue Group and that they had been sent to get their horse. Ken called to them and told them to take their horse away. They slowly emerged from behind the tree and led their horse away by the tattered rope that was around its scrawny neck. Ken felt sorry for the children and the horse. All was not well in the Blue Group.

There was a petition going around about charging the Blue Group with expenses incurred by the villagers in cleaning up after their horses and the trail of garbage left wherever they went in the village. Many had signed it and there was a growing frustration against the group that was increasing daily. These people were troublesome in many ways and the villagers wanted them gone. One night a large group of people from all of the groups gathered in a circle around the commune. They held torches and a proclamation against their habitation in the village environs was read out presumably for the Blue Group to hear and obey. None of the Blue Group emerged from their tent. The proclamations were mostly against the health problems caused by the piling up of refuse and dung. Not one peep was heard from behind the tent walls. The group yelled long and loudly against the Blues but not one response was heard. Even the horses seemed to have disappeared. On closer inspection the tent was found to be empty! The Blues had disappeared! They had left a terrible mess. The crowd decided to burn everything down the next day after a warning had been issued once again about the necessity of their leaving. Ken witnessed all of this from the edge of the crowd. He wondered where the group had gone to and he didn't have to wonder for very long because when he got back to his house he found that the group had decided to camp in the garden he had so lovingly created!

There they were, everyone of them and their horses and all their luggage, equipment and wagons! Ken told them that they would have to leave immediately. Brother William approached Ken with a look of great weariness and sadness. Tears were welling up in his eyes. He implored Ken to assist his flock in their great time of need. They had run out of funds and now the town was against them. Ken ran to get Frank as he would know what to do in this situation. Frank came running along with some others and as they saw the situation there were cries of shock and amazement. Frank told Ken that these people were in great distress and that they would have to allow them to stay the night. Frank said that some of the elderly and children should be allowed to stay in the apartment community room. Ken thought that this was a good idea. The most needy were taken to the apartment building and the rest tried to make themselves comfortable in the garden. The residents gave them hot drinks and sandwiches and blankets. Ken allowed several children to spend the night in the extra bedroom he had in his house. He fed them and they gobbled up the food as if they hadn't eaten for a week. The children fell asleep right away. Ken did not sleep as he was wondering what in the world they could do for these people. There were about fifty of them along with about ten horses. Finally he fell asleep to the snorting of horses and the coughs of those outside in the dark garden.

The next day dawned bright and warm but Ken wasn't feeling so happy about this day. He had been awakened at the crack of dawn by horses rubbing against his house. He fed them some carrots and then he surveyed the garden. It was in a shambles! People were everywhere. Flowers had been trampled and bushes had been almost destroyed. As they woke up the people looked around at each other and many of them began to cry as they remembered the events that had led them to this place. Brother William thanked Ken for the generosity shown to his persecuted group. Open Arms residents had prepared breakfast for all them and it was being served in the community room. It was quite crowded but everyone seemed to be enjoying the healthy, nourishing food which was being served. The cinnamon buns were popular. There were smiles all around. After everyone had eaten their fill and the tables had been cleared Frank announced that there would be a meeting in that room in a few minutes and everyone could attend it. The meeting was going to be about what would happen next to the Blues (as they liked to be called).

Ken stood at the front entrance to the room and watched everyone get settled to await what would transpire next. Frank stood at the front of the room and made a surprising announcement. He told the group that he, as the owner of the apartments (Ken had not known this fact) had decided to have a vote from all apartment dwellers as to the possibility of the Blues having residence among them! He explained that accommodations would be tight but in the near future he would have a second apartment block built on the property. Everyone was surprised. The Blues looked very encouraged. The Open Arms people looked puzzled. Ken was wondering to himself as to where everyone would live until the new apartment was built. Frank went on to explain a plan he had for housing the nomading Blues. Every apartment would take one or two members. Families would be housed near one another and children kept with their families if possible. There was a low murmur in the crowd. Everyone had been taken aback by this turn of events. Frank then called for a vote. Surprisingly, the show of hands indicated that the Blues would be housed in the apartments. Ken had not voted as he thought this scheme was ridiculous. How would these people be looked after? Where was money going to come from to feed these extra mouths and how would their personal and medical needs be met? He also wondered what the rest of the village would think about this arrangement. Ken didn't want his world to be changed by these strange people. He didn't want them in the garden or even near his place. He stomped out of the room and went to his house.

By the end of the day every Blue Group member had a place to stay and all of them seemed quite settled. The horses had been taken to a nearby park and tethered until a plan for their care could be established. The Blue Group children took turns feeding them grass they had pulled up by the sides of the roads. Ken was still very upset by all of this and he kept to himself. Surely there would be trouble because of this turn of events. He found out all too soon that indeed there was big trouble brewing on the horizon.

The next day was sunny and bright and Ken was working in the garden when he suddenly found himself surrounded by people from the village. They asked him where the Blues were as they had heard that they all lived in the apartments now. Ken affirmed that they did indeed live in the apartments. At that very instant, several members of the Blue Group were seen hanging up their clothes on a clothesline that had been strung up for them by the back entrance. The villagers raced over to them. Ken did not follow but he heard them shouting at the astonished Blues. Arms and voices were raised against the Blues who retreated quickly into the building. The villagers stamped away mumbling threats. An hour later, a huge group composed of many of the various groups came back with big signs. Ken watched them march around the apartment building yelling out against the Blues. He noticed the Purple group there and he looked for Star and her Mother but he couldn't tell if they were in among all the throng. The Purple group was carrying a banner on silver poles which proclaimed the Rule of Law. The Yellow group, as usual was laughing their heads off and doing cartwheels and making fools of themselves. The residents of the apartment were beginning to look out of the windows at the spectacle before them.

Apparently, the mob was disturbed about the living arrangements in the apartment. Of course the horses were another problem. Overcrowding and village by-laws were being broken. The Mayor of the Village of Wonder appeared and warned, through a megaphone, that the local health and social welfare personnel were going to be notified about the many breeches of the law that were taking place in and around the apartment. That announcement stirred the crowd to new heights of yelling and fist waving. The Mayor warned that the local police would be coming with eviction notices if the Blues weren't gone by the next day. The expenses caused by the Blues would also have to be paid in full! Everyone cheered and marched around the apartment a few times and then left marching and singing a song of victory.

Ken wondered what was going to happen next. He wandered over to the apartment and went to Frank's rooms where he found him all alone staring into the garden. Ken asked him what would happen to these people. Frank looked very sad. He had so wanted to help them but now it seemed that the group would not be able to stay and that they'd have to go on their weary way to nowhere. Frank really cared about these strange people. Ken marveled at this and wondered why he didn't feel much compassion for them. It bothered him that he was quite selfish. This whole episode had shown him that he wasn't a very nice person at times. He felt ashamed. This was an ugly revelation and he felt he should help somehow and he asked Frank what he could do for these people.

Frank told Ken that he had a plan that would possibly help to keep the Blue Group in the apartment building. He would invite the inspection authorities to view all the individual apartments and the living conditions of these people. He was sure that they wouldn't find anything wrong. He asked Ken to set up some cots in some of the apartments and to buy some bedding that day. He also gave him some minor repair jobs to do in some of the apartments. Ken was glad to help and hoped that his contributions would somehow help the situation. He got busy with his tasks and before long it was getting dark and so he headed toward his little house. He met Brother William taking a solitary stroll in the garden. He waved in a friendly manner. Brother William waved back and resumed his slow pace with his head lowered, deep in thought. Ken didn't want to intrude into his nocturnal musings but he guessed that the man was deeply troubled. Ken went into his little home and Echo meowed a hello. She was getting big and she had the habit of often prowling around at night in the garden. Ken suspected that she would have kittens soon. She wanted out and so Ken let her go on her merry way into the night.

The Inspectors came the next day and snooped around for about an hour. Members from the various Groups hung around outside the building, yelling and making a big commotion. The members of the Blue Group were trying their best to smile and accommodate the officials. They had dressed in their best and were clean and presentable. They looked healthier and happier, thanks to the care of the residents. The Inspectors summoned everyone together after they had thoroughly checked out the living quarters of everyone in the Group. What they had to say was very unexpected.

The Inspectors declared without any equivocation that the residents appeared to be situated in a satisfactory manner! However, they wanted the Blue Group to be moved within three months. Their horses would have to be sent to a farm as the park was unsuitable for them. There was a nearby farm that would accept the horses for a fee. After that declaration the Inspectors left suddenly. Everyone was beaming in delight! The only problem was the horses and how money could be obtained to stable them at the farm. Frank had the idea that members of the Group could work for the farmer. He would check into that possibility. He also announced that he thought that a second apartment building could be constructed within the three month period if everyone chipped in to help in whatever ways they could manage. There was a chorus of cheers as everyone laughed and clapped and hugged one another. The people outside the building wondered what all this was about and they started peering through the windows. Frank went outside to tell them the news and the crowd muttered and mumbled and threatened and then, they too, left.

That night there was a huge celebration supper and the whole apartment community, Ken included, sat down to eat in the community room. Brother William was beaming and declared that the Open Arms people were saints. They all looked at each other with little smiles. He promised that his people would work hard on the new building and that several men had volunteered to work on the farm. The children sang a song for everyone. Ken couldn't quite make it out but it was about blue water and bluebells in the land of the great blue heron. Everyone clapped politely and all were given huge pieces of chocolate cake. There had never been any dissent between the Blues and The Open Arms people. They all got along so well and it seemed that they had all lived together forever. Little groups chattered as the children ran around with chocolate smeared on their faces and elsewhere! Ken went home pleased with himself. He was glad that he had had some part in helping these people.

The townspeople were not amused at all by the continued residence of the Blue Group in the apartment building. The Open Arms people had never been really accepted by the village and now they were being persecuted for harboring the troublesome, strange people dressed in blue. The members of other Groups didn't think that they themselves were odd in any way at all. The next day a large group came and threw eggs at the building and they shouted for an hour. There was no police back up. Finally, the mob left and all was peaceful.

Some of the Blues cleaned up the building. Ken went about his duties and helped out the new residents by going to the village for food and provisions for them. Frank had opened up an account at the local Bank for their needs. Ken wondered why Frank seemed to have lots of money. It occurred to him that he knew very little about the man. He was thinking about this as he drove Frank's truck into the village. As he parked the truck in the parking lot of the Food Basket, a group or people surrounded it and stood silently staring at him. He tried to pretend that they weren't there but they started to block his way into the store. He decided that he'd come back later and he got back into the truck and drove away down the street to the Bank. There was no mob there and so Ken was able withdraw money with no problem other than a few stares and some whispering. Ken felt uncomfortable and left hurriedly. He went back to the Food Basket and fortunately the crowd had dispersed. He ordered a mound of groceries and stuffed the back of the truck with them. He drove quickly back to the apartment. Everyone available pitched in to unload and deliver the food to the various families. They were so grateful and several residents invited Ken to dine with them. He politely declined but promised he'd dine with them in the future.

Chapter Five
Strange Activities

Ken had not forgotten his quest of hiking up White Mountain. He felt that he had to get away and so a hike would be the ticket. He prepared a lunch and took a water bottle, said goodbye to a chubby Echo and set forth on his adventure. After about half an hour he reached the path which would take him up the mountain. At least he thought that this was the way up to the heights. After a few minutes on the path which was well-worn by other Groups (which had all failed in their attempts), Ken noticed a glint of something through the trees to his right. He started toward it and as he neared it he saw that it was a gate. This was very unexpected in the middle of a forest. Indeed it was a tall, iron gate. It was just standing there unattached to anything.

Ken reached out to open the gate's latch and suddenly a loud thunderous noise sounded throughout the forest. Ken froze with his hand in the air, not knowing what to do next. After a minute the sound stopped and all was still. He wondered if he should try to open the gate. Slowly he reached forward to unlock the latch. Again the sound came and again Ken stood there not knowing what was going to happen. The sound died away and Ken thought that he'd just go around the gate instead of opening it but that didn't work either. The sound came as soon as his foot started to pass by the side of the gate. It was getting late and Ken decided that he'd go home and try again another day.

None of the other Groups had ever mentioned the gate to Ken in their discussions at the community center. Star, who had become his confidante, had not heard of it either. She wanted to see it and so the two of them decided that they'd go together to see it a few days later. Star had become very disillusioned with the Purple Group especially after the fiasco with the Blue Group. She was ashamed by the way the Blues had been treated by her Group as well as by the other Groups. Her mother had directed some of the attacks against the outcast Blues and Star was very upset with her and all the rules her Group kept coming up with and which were impossible to follow. She had decided to move out of her home and she was now living in a small house near the center of the village. Fortunately, she was able to get a good rental deal and a job at The Delicious Cookie as a baker's assistant. After all, she told Ken, she was old enough to be on her own and it was time that she became more independent. She had also vowed to leave the Purple Group and never get attached again to any Group. Ken thought she had made the right decisions.

It was a wonderful day in April when the two friends ventured forth towards White Mountain Trail (as it had been named by the locals). Ken was very happy to have such a pretty, friendly companion. As they came down the trail Ken motioned to Star to look to her right and there was the gate. However, to their great surprise it was open! This was very strange! Hesitantly, they walked toward the open gate and then bravely, Star went first and nothing happened. Ken followed and safely joined Star on the other side of the gate. They both looked at each other in wonderment. There seemed to be no one else around. They walked forward and suddenly the gate clanged shut! Now they were scared and wished to be miles way from this strange place. How were they going to get back home? They decided to run around the side of the gate and not stop until they had left the forest. They joined hands and ran by the gate and down the trail until they got out the forest. There was no sound. They stopped to catch their breaths and sat down by the side of the road that led to the village. Maybe the wind had shut the gate. Maybe the noises heard previously had just been a coincidence. These thoughts ran through Ken's head. Maybe some of the Groups did use the gate. Maybe he shouldn't worry about it as it all could be explained. Star wanted to go home and so the two adventurers parted with the promise that they'd try again after a few weeks had passed.

Ken kept thinking about that gate and what significance it had, if any, in regards to the quest to hike up White Mountain. He asked Frank if he had ever heard of a gate and he said that he'd heard some talk about some of the Groups encountering it in recent months. It hadn't kept them from forging past it but then again, no one had got to the peak of White Mountain, either. Who would set up a gate in the middle of a forest? It just didn't make sense. Ken asked Frank if anyone had lived on the lower slopes of that mountain. Frank had sat silent for a few moments and then he told Ken that there had been a hermit living on the outskirts of the town about five years ago. He was seen everywhere but he had no fixed address and he was so peculiar that the villagers called him Wild Tom. This man had the strangest glare and he only ate fruit and nuts. Sometimes he was called Nutty Fruitcake and this was because he had the "habit" of stealing nuts and fruit from the grocery store. Where he got the little money he had, no one knew for sure. Ken couldn't imagine that Wild Tom would set up a tall gate in the forest.

As Ken was mowing the lawn a few days later, Frank came up to him and said that he had remembered something about Wild Tom. Ken and Frank sat on the bench near the rose arbor and they fell into a deep conversation. Frank told Ken something that helped him to begin to imagine what might have occurred in that part of the forest where the gate had been placed. Wild Tom had bragged that he had found gold but no had paid any attention to him. He spent a lot of time on the lower part of White Mountain. He claimed that he had started a gold mine. This was not believed and so everyone left him alone to do whatever he was doing up there. Ken thought that maybe Wild Tom had discovered something on the mountain. Who had erected the gate? Surely Wild Tom couldn't have done that with his meager means and lack of friendly supporters. What had happened to him? Frank said that Wild Tom just disappeared and was not heard of anymore around the village. Ken wondered if Wild Nutty Fruitcake Tom had met an untimely death. His mind swirled with possibilities and played out scenarios as to what could have happened to that man.

True to their plans, Ken and Star set out to uncover the mystery of the gate. They were determined to explore the area thoroughly and not to run away at the first noise. Resolutely they approached the gate. It was shut and all was quiet in the forest. Only birds sang and little creatures stirred in the underbrush. Together they went through the gate and shut it behind themselves. Then they went on into the forest for about half a mile. As they walked along looking at the trees that soared into the blue sky, they suddenly stopped in their tracks. The sound that Ken had heard before came thundering through the trees and then stopped. Star looked at Ken and then they both continued on as they had planned. They weren't going to run home this time. Gradually other sounds came filtering out of the forest. There was something going on and the two curious adventurers wanted to know exactly what was taking place in this forest. They pushed through the foliage without stopping until they came to the edge of a clearing. They ducked down and peered from behind a wide fir tree and to their astonishment they saw a Group there! It was the Brown Group and they were all very busy with wheelbarrows and pick axes and there were tents set up and children running around. It seemed to be meal time as everyone was gathering around a long rough hewn table where pots and plates of food had been placed. Ken and Star could not believe their eyes! This seemed to be a well-organized endeavor which must have been going on for some time. They noticed a road leading out of the clearing and wonder of wonders there was a huge gravel truck parked on it.

Everyone sat down on stumps of logs and ate heartily and it was a happy scene to watch from a distance. Their conversations could not be heard very well and so the two "spies" crept forward on their hands and knees to hear what was being discussed. They could only hear a few words. They were able to hear something about a schedule and crews and the word "gold" was repeated often. Ken wondered if these people were mining for gold nearby. Star whispered that she thought that this was a mining operation. Ken nodded. After the meal, the men got up and gathered tools and wheel barrows and headed into the forest. Thankfully, it was not in the direction where Ken and Star were hiding. The ladies cleaned up and the children helped too. Then they all went into their tents for a siesta of sorts. Not a sound was heard after a while. The two adventurers crept closer to the camp. They came to an enormous dumpster. Ken was able to climb up and look inside it and to his surprise he saw what appeared to be rocks with white flecks in them. Star signaled that someone was coming down the road towards the truck. They hid behind the dumpster and watched what would occur next. They didn't have long to wait.

A tall man climbed up into the truck and he sat in the cab as if he was waiting for something or someone. About twenty minutes passed and then a disturbance was heard as the men came back to the clearing. They were all pushing wheelbarrows full of the same kind of rocks as Ken had seen in the dumpster. The truck's tailgate was opened up and the men shoveled their rocks into it as fast as was possible. The women and children appeared and pitched in to help. Soon there was a high heap of rocks in the truck. Some of the men came to the dumpster and opened one end and began to fill their wheelbarrows with the rocks and then they pushed them towards the truck where the rocks were pitched in to be added to the increasing rock pile. The dumpster was gradually emptied and the truck was filled and it then backed down the road and disappeared. It was dark by now and Ken and Star had seen enough for one day and so they scurried back to the gate and down the path and came to the road that led to the village. They were thinking over all that they had witnessed that day and then they said good-bye under the full moon.

Chapter Six
Golden Dreams

Ken was amazed by what they had seen. The next day he asked Frank if he knew anything about gold mining. Of course he did. Frank was a fount of knowledge. Ken told him what he had seen the day before. Frank raised his eyebrows in interest. He wanted to know every detail about what had occurred there in the clearing. He told Ken that the rocks probably had quartz mixed with gold in them and they were probably having them taken to some site which would break down the rocks in the hope of finding gold in them. Frank thought that the operation in the clearing was quite crude but he wondered how they had been able to get so much rock out of wherever they were working. He mused about what whether they were drilling or pounding or just hacking away at the rocks. He concluded it was probably a very unsophisticated operation. Frank was so curious about all this that he wanted to go with Ken to observe these goings - on for himself. The mystery of Wild Tom was still on Ken's mind. He thought that somehow this strange man was a part of this activity on White Mountain.

As it was a warm day, the two friends set out without jackets and only water bottles. Soon they were on the Trail and headed towards the gate. Frank looked at the gate carefully before going through it with Ken following close behind him. It didn't take long to find the clearing as loud noises such as Ken had heard before were assaulting their ears. They had to cover them a few times. Ken thought they sounded like explosions. This time the two men would try to discover where the men went to find their rocks. To their surprise there were no tents, women or children in the clearing. There wasn't a trace of anything left except for the dumpster. Quickly they ran over to the area that Ken had seen the men come from with their wheelbarrows full of rocks. There was a well-worn narrow path leading deeper into the forest. They had climbed this path for about half a mile when they heard men's voices and creeping closer they could see a group of them at the mouth of a cave. It was a huge opening in the side of the mountain. Sure enough, explosives were being set up for another blast inside the "mine". Frank and Ken moved back further into the forest and ducked down ready for the explosion. When all was ready, a tremendous blast shook the whole area. The men went into the cave, no doubt to see what they had unearthed. Frank and Ken crept closer again and could see no one around the cave and so they were emboldened to advance closer to the mouth of the cave. The men inside could not be heard and so the two 'spies' ventured into the entrance. There were rocks everywhere. There was smoke which made Ken and Frank cough. Not a sound was heard. It was pitch black and they were stepping in water. They felt their way by keeping close to the walls. There was light ahead and as they got closer they could hear men talking but it was unclear as to what was being discussed.

There beside flickering flashlights they saw about ten men talking together. There was a huge pile of rocks blocking the way forward. Obviously this was a very amateur and quite possibly dangerous operation. Frank motioned to Ken to go back and so the two men picked their way back to the entrance of the cave. The bright sun was overpowering to them as they stumbled out of the cave and tore away as fast as possible back to the gate and onto the Trail and then onto the road home. They were dirty, hungry, scratched and bruised but they had made it out of there before the men caught them snooping into their operation.

Back at Frank's place the two friends were able to relax after they had washed up and had some food. As they sipped coffee Frank mused that this operation was environmentally not friendly, dangerous and he was surprised that the Brown Group were involved in it. He thought that it was quite possibly illegal as permits and surveys and Governmental approval were all part of mining ventures. Frank was clearly troubled by what he had witnessed that day. Ken still wondered how this had all been going on without anyone in the village gossiping about it as they always did about any occurrences or juicy news.

Frank told Ken the next day that he would have to go to the leader of the Brown Group and ask him about his activities at the cave. He wanted to make sure that this was legal and safe for all concerned. Ken said that he thought that it wasn't legal and it definitely wasn't safe as they all appeared to pretend that they were miners. He couldn't figure why they would destroy the environment as they were the ones who were always trying to protect it. He told Frank that he'd go with him to the leader's home the next day. Frank agreed and they planned to leave at ten in the morning. That evening Ken went to Star's house as she had invited him to supper. She had some news for him. She told Ken that she wanted to have a career and that working in a bakery wasn't her dream job. As she had always loved children, she had decided that she wanted to train to become a teacher and hopefully some day return to Wonder as a teacher in the elementary school. She had just received money from an Uncle's estate and so she was making plans to attend the University of Monsa in September. Ken was taken aback by this news as he had come to rely on his friendship with Star. He sat in silence at Star's kitchen table looking at the spaghetti in front of him and not knowing what to say to her. She looked glum and they both sat there for a few moments. Ken summoned up a bright face and told Star that he was happy for her and that he'd miss her tremendously. She told him that she'd visit often and that they'd keep in touch. Four years away seemed so long and Ken said very little after that and then he left about ten minutes later saying good-bye and giving Star a hug.

On his way home Ken remembered that he had forgotten to tell Star about his latest adventures with Frank. He'd tell her all the news after the meeting with John Blair, who was the leader of the Brown Group. He went to bed thinking about what it would be like to have Star gone and far away for months on end. He felt sad. Finally, he drifted off to sleep and had a dream that an explosion blasted the whole cave apart and miraculously no one was hurt. The cave was closed permanently and no more mining operations took place on the mountain.

Ken woke up the next morning wondering if the dream was true and then realized that the activities on White Mountain were really taking place and that he'd be talking to John Blair that very day. The day was cloudy and rainy and as Ken went over to Frank's apartment, he was pleased to note that the construction of the new apartment building was coming along quite well. The workmen were hammering away even in the rain. Frank wanted this building up by the end of the summer. Ken waved to Brother William who was sitting on a bench in the garden. He was looking at the workmen with a pleased look on his thin face. He told Ken that the building was going to be perfect for his flock. Ken smiled and nodded and went to find Frank.

Frank and Ken went in the truck to the Brown Group's section of the village. It was strangely deserted. Not a soul, dog or cat was to be seen on the street. Ken thought that they might all be at the mine. No one was at home at the leader's place. They knocked on a few more doors but no one answered. Were they there and hiding or were they on the mountain? Frank and Ken decided to go back to the mining operation. This time they would take camping gear with them as they planned to stay overnight to try and get a better idea as to just what was happening there on that mountain.

It was later on that afternoon that Ken and Frank found themselves in a bushy area where they had decided to camp out and use as a base for their explorations. They could safely view everything from their vantage point. Sure enough the whole Brown Group seemed to be there and all seemed very excited about something. A crowd of people encircled several men who were talking to them. The crowd erupted into shouting and laughter several times as the men continued to speak about something that the onlookers could not clearly discern. One of the speakers held up a boulder and the crowd cheered. Ken and Frank inched closer and closer being careful not to be seen by anyone. Little did they know that they themselves were being viewed by eyes in the forest behind them.

Frank and Ken could hear the voices now and they were talking about the big discovery of another seam found that day and they were showing samples that they had taken out of it. They were declaring that this was yet another discovery that would make them all very wealthy. More cheers erupted from the crowd. It was now dark and the crowd was dispersing to tents and so the two men went back their camp. As they crawled through the bushes they saw flashes of light to their right. They slowly and carefully crawled towards them and to their surprise they saw another camp with people sitting together with only one large flashlight to keep total darkness away from them. Ken could not guess who they might be as it was very difficult to see anything clearly. Frank motioned to Ken to head back to their camp.

When they got to their camp they were surprised to find that someone had tried to mess things up as if to leave a message that they had been discovered. Frank told Ken that they should leave right away as things could get ugly if they stayed overnight. Ken agreed and the two of them, as quietly as possible, proceeded to quickly exit the forest and then they headed home under a full moon. They were both exhausted when they arrived home. They agreed that they'd meet for breakfast at Ken's place the next morning to make plans. Ken's head was whirling as he tried to figure out who knew what about what was going on there on White Mountain. He tossed and turned all night. Once he woke up as Echo's kitten, Daisy, jumped onto his pillow. The other kittens had been given away but Daisy had been kept. She was always into some mischief. Ken finally woke up several hours later and started breakfast. Frank came and the two sat down to eat and discuss what they should do next.

The two men mused as to what groups knew about the mine. Maybe there were many groups all working together or apart to get in on the mine's treasures. This was a dangerous situation and Frank decided he was going to go to the authorities about this situation. Many people, not to mention children, could get seriously hurt. They agreed that they would not approach the mining area until the authorities had been notified. Ken was getting very nervous about would happen after the authorities had been notified about what was happening on White Mountain.

True to his word, Frank went to the village office to talk to the Mayor. Mayor Bill Wallace was someone who did not belong to any of the Groups. Since he had been elected a year previously, he had discouraged new Groups from settling around or in Wonder. No new Groups had been allowed entrance into the community under his watch except for the Blue Group. Somehow that Group had slipped in but they had been dealt with in a satisfactory manner (so he thought). Frank entered into the Mayor's office and sat down in a big red chair facing the jovial Mayor Bill. They joked about recent village events and they talked about the Blue Group. Then the Mayor asked Frank what he had on his mind.

As Frank told the Mayor about all that he had seen and heard about the activities on White Mountain, the Mayor's eyes widened in astonishment. His face got red and he shifted in his chair. After Frank had finished his report, Mayor Bill stood up and looked out of the window which, coincidentally faced White Mountain. He spun around and faced Frank. He was visibly upset and angry. He told Frank that all this activity was highly illegal. He would send up mining officials that very day to inspect the mine. He would also send all of his police force (which was small) as well. All of the people there would be evicted and the mountain would be off limits except to the authorities. He said that he would be sure to tell his officials to be careful not to cause undue anxiety or harm to anyone. He thanked Frank profusely for reporting this situation. As Frank left the office, the Mayor was on the phone in deep conversation and barking out orders. Frank felt reassured that all would be handled in a safe and legal manner. He was about to be greatly disappointed.

Frank went back to his home and told Ken about the meeting with the Mayor. Ken felt reassured and he hoped that all would go well on the mountain. He busied himself with his various maintenance jobs for the rest of the day. About five o'clock, as he was entering his little house, he heard a tremendous explosion coming from the mountain area. Several explosions followed. Ken was very anxious as he knew it was happening on White Mountain. He guessed that all was not going according to plan on the mountain. He ran to Frank's, where they assembled some first aid supplies and the two of them drove in the truck to the foot of the mountain. The treed area was covered in blue smoke. Several people were straggling out of the forest. Ken raced back to town to get medical help and people from the Open Arms. Frank stayed back to help the people who had struggled to get away from the blasts. They told him that many had been injured and that the mine had erupted into a giant cauldron of fire and smoke. While the officials were inspecting the mine, it exploded. Ken had his cell phone with him and he called the Mayor's office to request immediate assistance.

Chapter Seven
Backlash

Over the next several hours, the survivors of the blasts were found and treated. All of the officials and some of the miners had been killed. It was hard to search for people in the dark and so the emergency team decided to come back the next day for further searches. Thankfully, no children had died. Many children and their parents however, had to be taken to the hospital. Some were so badly burned that they had to be flown to Monsa. Helicopters were landing every few hours. Frank, Ken and members of the Blue Group and the Open Arms people worked tirelessly to assist the victims of this terrible disaster.

By the next morning all of the remaining victims had been accounted for and had been treated. The whole area had been taped off because it was a police investigation site. Ken was exhausted and so he spent the rest of the day trying to catch up on his lost sleep. Daisy and Echo slept at the foot of his bed. It was evening when he woke and he was disoriented. Then the scenes of hurt and crying people came to his mind. He felt guilty that he hadn't reported the activities on the mountain sooner. Perhaps, people would not have died. Ken dragged himself out of his bed, sending the cats scurrying away, meowing over the disturbance to their peace. He walked into the garden and saw Star sitting on a bench near the rose trellis. She looked lost and bewildered. Ken greeted her and they just sat together there until the darkness came and surrounded them. Star told Ken that she would be going to the city the next day to arrange for her boarding needs and to register for her courses. Ken told her that he'd be sorry to have her leave the village. That was all he could think of to tell her as he was tongue tied. Star assured him that she'd keep in touch. They hugged each other and then ... Star walked away into the darkness. Ken's eyes threatened to produce many tears but he forced himself back to his house. He would miss Star so much!

The late summer weeks were a blur of investigations, meetings and criminal trials in the city. The whole story was finally coming out and it was worse that anyone could have imagined. Nutty Tom had discovered the gold mine. He had set up the gate to mark an entrance area for himself but he hadn't accounted for others finding it and the mine. Apparently, human bones had been found near the entrance to the mine and they were being analyzed. Everyone thought that they belonged to Tom. The Brown Group was being represented by a team of lawyers as The Brown Group members were the prime suspects in the disappearance of Nutty Tom. They weren't talking. Other groups weren't talking either but gossip floated around that at least two other groups had been involved in the mine fiasco. Everyone stayed in their own 'camps' with little communication but a lot of speculation was engaged in at every gathering. The trial date had been set for the end of September. It would actually be held in Wonder. All were on pins and needles as to what would happen at the trial.

No one was allowed to move out of Wonder unless there was an emergency or a dire circumstance. Some of the groups wanted to leave but this wasn't possible. Tempers flared as people who didn't want to live in Wonder had to continue to exist there in their unhappiness. The ban on moving out was set to continue until the end of December or when the trial was finished; whichever came first. This was one of many backlashes that had occurred because of the mine disaster. Everyone was suspicious of everyone else. The only happy people were those in the Open Arms community. The other groups had been grateful for their help during the explosion. Even the Blue Group had gained some status due to their swift assistance on that terrible day and on the following, agony-filled days. The Open Arms community was trying to reach out to the various groups by providing necessities and visiting families in their homes. They tried to bring hope and comfort to the recovering victims in the hospital.

An evacuation plan was secretly being concocted by two groups. These were the guilty groups. They had been in on the mining scheme together. The Brown Group and the Green Group had set about trying to mine the mountain. They had always bragged that they were all for protecting the Earth. Now they had destroyed the mountain and many lives had been lost. There was some suspicion as to who knew what about the demise of Nutty Tom. The two groups were meeting secretly and arranging a mass exodus. All together they numbered about one hundred and twenty people. They planned to leave very early in the morning on the last day of August. They had even reserved a large camping group space in a National Forest campsite about fifty miles away to the north.

Quietly the families got into their vehicles with the necessities for travel but they were also leaving behind their lives. Their homes would be filled with furniture and personal possessions which they never planned to see again. The time of departure was three-thirty in the morning under a full moon. The children were sleepy as they were put into the vehicles. Slowly the vehicles crawled away down the darkened streets of the village they had all been a part of for many years. No one spoke as they all headed north to the unknown. They were on the run and they hadn't really thought about what would happen because they did not want to stay and be convicted of crimes they may or may not have committed. So far they had not been detected. As they rolled north the adults sat, dozed or drove toward the mystery of their futures. The children slept deeply not worrying as they had been told a story about where they were going and as far as they knew it was to be an adventurous holiday. The sun was starting to peek over the eastern horizon as the cars, vans and trucks turned onto the gravel road that led to the campground.

The gates would open at six. The long line of vehicles waited at the gate until it was opened. They were ushered in by a sleepy attendant who must have wondered at their numbers. The groups found their camping sites and started to set up tents and to unload their possessions. They tried to be quiet and to not disturb the other campers. Some of the children woke up and were making loud noises about being hungry and some were grouchy and complaining. Soon other campers were yelling at them to be quiet. The children were hushed but they didn't like that and soon they were making lots of commotion. Campers started to emerge from their tents and some were threatening to tell the authorities. The two groups started breakfast for their members. The chief cooks and organizational types got things moving along at a quick pace and before very long the children were happily munching on pancakes and various egg dishes, washed down by milk. The other campers were also eating and so a peace of sorts had developed. But that was not to last for long.

About nine o'clock two police cars entered the campgrounds. The two groups knew that they were in huge trouble. Everyone tried to pretend that the authorities weren't there in their midst as they sat around the campfires and joked with one another all the while keeping an eye on the fast approaching officers. They greeted the officers politely. They told huge fibs through their smiling mouths and it looked like they were going to get away with their cunning trickery. The officers had been telephoned by the attendant that the groups had come into the campgrounds at an early hour and upset the other campers. The officers turned towards the group leaders and took them off further away from everyone to interrogate them in depth. Meanwhile, the other group members were marshalling themselves for an exodus. Quietly, they wandered into the forest in small groups or individually until all had melted away. The group leaders came back from the questioning by the police to find that their members had seemingly vanished. The police had left but had warned them that if any more trouble was reported that they'd be back in a flash. Apparently, the police had not heard of the escape of the groups from Wonder. The group leaders headed toward the forest to look for their lost "lambs".

Chapter Eight
Lost and Found

By that evening the groups had been rounded up by their leaders and all were on the road again minus some needed provisions which had been left at the campgrounds. Several days of scrambling for food and trying to stay out of sight was causing great stress for the groups. All were exhausted, dirty and hungry. They wished that they had never left Wonder. They were low on the necessities of life and there was no where to go but further into remote wilderness areas. One night they discovered a hamlet near a mountain lake. It was called Frog Lagoon. There were only a few hundred people living there and they seemed very friendly. The groups decided that this would be a good place to stay if the people accepted them. This hamlet was so out of touch with the wider world that it didn't have televisions or even radios but this was a point of pride for them as they wanted to live untouched as much as possible from the world. This was perfect for the groups and they were accepted quite quickly. Soon they all were living in harmony together. The groups had been given some land to start building homes. All the villagers pitched in to help build them and they shared their own homes with the newcomers until the homes were finished. Winter would be coming and so all worked hard to finish up the homes before the first snow fell. The men of the groups found work in local sawmills. Everything was going so well and the groups began to feel safe from any discovery by the authorities.

Ken and a posse of people from Wonder were on the road looking for the groups. The last place that the police had seen them was at the campgrounds. Ken's group arrived there about two days after the groups had left the campground. By that time there was a full scale alert warning about these fugitives. At the campground Ken was amazed to find so many things that had been left behind. The search party visited many of the towns around the area and asked questions about the groups but they found no real clues. The posse returned to Wonder and disbanded.

Several months later, based on new information, another posse set out to search again. This information set them on a course that would land them in Frog Lagoon. Ken's party advanced slowly down the dirt road which led to the village. He had warned the local police as to their whereabouts and to be prepared to come as backup when the signal was given that the groups had been found.

It was evening and all was quiet in the village. Smoke curled up from the chimneys as supper was being prepared in many homes. Ken and his small band crept to a window of the nearest home and looked in on a happy scene of many children, adults and some pets all crowded together in blissful accord. Everyone came to a long table and sat down and then they began to receive hot bowls of stew and huge white buns. The children washed down the buns with milk while the adults drank coffee or tea. There was a lot of laughter and banter. Ken could not believe his eyes when he picked out many familiar faces all seemingly entrenched in this new community. How had they done it? He realized that he'd need a lot of police assistance in getting all of these people located as they were probably living in many other homes. Ken went to other homes and saw similar scenes of domestic tranquility. These people were like leeches that had landed in a new place and sucked all they wanted out of gullible, unsophisticated people. What would happen when things didn't go their way? Would it be a repeat of the doings on White Mountain? Ken thought he knew the answer to that frightening question.

Ken and his men decided to retreat to their vehicles for the night. Ken phoned the police and they agreed to meet them in the morning. Ken had difficulty sleeping in Frank's truck. Frank was too busy with the new apartment building and so he had lent his truck to Ken. Ken had taken some of the Blue Group men along with him on this search for the escapees. They had taken another truck. Ken's truck was full of supplies for the journey. Ken couldn't stop wondering what would happen the next day. He tossed and turned on the back seat of the truck. Finally he dozed off to sleep about three in the morning.

At dawn Ken was awakened by tapping on his window. The other men had already got up and were ready for action. Ken roused himself and they all sat in the other truck and ate a hasty breakfast of dried up doughnuts and some orange juice. There were murmurs about why they hadn't thought to get some coffee at that last town. They could have put it into their thermos bottles. After some more grumbling they all started to talk about what was going to happen that day. Ken had confirmed with the police that they would all meet together at the spot where they now were camped. The police said that they'd arrive at eight-thirty that morning. All eyes were glued to the road to see if the police cars were coming down it towards them.

Sure enough, seven police vehicles, which included some vans, came slowly down the dusty road as the sun climbed in the sky. It was probably going to be a long, hot September day. The yellow and orange leaves on the trees made the scene somewhat bizarre as it was such a perfect day and something which could be very imperfect could take place. All the men and the one lone policewoman stood around their vehicles talking to Ken's posse. The plan was set and the time for action was announced by an older policeman with a red, round face. At noon they would all hide in several pre-determined places and enter the settlement when told to advance. The policewoman would go first and call everyone together by using her bullhorn and ask about the whereabouts of a wanted man who may be in their midst. There was no man. This was a ruse to get everyone all together in one place. She would radio her position back to the officer in charge.

All went as planned and before one o'clock all the people were rounded up and standing in front of the town post office. The only problem was that the groups were mixed up with the townspeople and Ken wasn't sure who belonged to who and no one was talking. He was able to pick out about two dozen people but the rest he wasn't sure of and the policemen were getting impatient. As the sun set behind the blue hills, the groups finally decided that they'd better all confess and so by eight o'clock most of the ring leaders had been hauled off to the next city. Their group members would leave the next day for Wonder with police escorts. Ken was exhausted. He hadn't eaten anything all day and he slumped into his truck and fell asleep. He awoke when his truck started to move back and forth.

Ken woke up only to see the back of the biggest bear he had ever seen! It was rubbing against the truck. Perhaps it had an itch. Ken thought he could scare it away and so he started to shout at it. The bear turned around and stared at him with its beady eyes. It licked the window and started to paw at it. The bear could see and smell the food in the truck! Ken kept yelling and some of the searchers came running at the bear and it lumbered away into the forest. Ken was shaking but relieved that he'd be fine. They all decided it was time to head back to Wonder. Ken never wanted to come back to this weird place.

After an uneventful trip home Ken was so glad to get away from traveling and to return to his regular schedule. Ken learned that all the groups had left Wonder and the only remaining group was the Yellow Group which kept to itself and didn't get involved in community events. New people had moved into the village and they weren't a part of a group as far as Ken could discern. The leaders of the "mining groups" were tried and found guilty and sent off to jail. Their followers never returned to Wonder as a result many homes were left vacant. A huge garage sale was held and money was given to the community for local improvements for such things as roads, playgrounds and support for hospital upgrades. After all the turmoil of the last few years Wonder seemed to settle into some sense of normalcy. The Blue group had decided to abandon their cause and they now were part of the Open Arms community. They didn't wear blue and sadly their leader had died from a fall off of a ladder. No new leader had emerged and so the group had abandoned its quest. They all lived in the new apartment complex and worked in and around the community. Gone were the days of parades and roaming horses. They had integrated into the village life and they now were accepted as upstanding citizens. All in all, Wonder seemed to be rid of the craziness of its past and was looking forward to a bright future. However, that was not to be as forces were at work which would create chaos, confusion and confrontations.

Chapter Nine
False Worship

Christmas was approaching and Ken was excited because Star was coming home for a brief visit. His plan was to spend as much time with her as was possible and so his little home underwent a thorough cleaning and food and supplies were purchased. As Ken had become a "chef" of sorts, he was planning on creating yummy desserts and main courses. It was hoped that these "creations" would show off his culinary skills and hopefully this would impress Star. Fresh snow had fallen and it was a crisp, cool day with a blue sky. The sun shone on the snow, creating blue shadows and sparkling snow mounds. The Open Arms people also planned to invite Star to their homes and offer her some of their baking. The former blue group lived in their new Bright Hope Apartments. They also wanted to visit with Star. Everyone's favorite was Ken and they considered Star to be his true love. This embarrassed him as he wasn't sure about that but she definitely was a friend. There was a lot of teasing about Star.

One day about a week before Christmas Ken noticed something strange on White Mountain. It appeared to be white smoke ascending to the sky about half way up the mountain. No one had climbed that mountain since the mining tragedy and no one believed that truth was to be found up there anymore. What was going on? Ken hoped against hope that another strange group had not camped up there or were exploring up there for some mysterious purpose. He kept an eye on the mountain for several days. The smoke kept appearing periodically over the next few days. He wondered why someone would be up there in the cold snow. His curiosity got the best of him and he planned to explore the mountain.

It was two days before Christmas. Star was supposed to arrive that evening. Ken decided that he would get an early start and climb up the mountain to that area and take a quick look around and then hurry back as fast as possible. He packed a few supplies and bundled up against the cold wind that was whipping up the snowdrifts. He got to the mountain about nine o'clock and immediately started climbing. He noticed that there was a well-worn path with boot prints clearly left behind. He was able to make good progress and about ten he was nearing a clearing where he saw a huge fire with several people around it. Here we go again, was Ken's thought. Some more kooks were on the mountain and by the looks of what he saw, strange activities were taking place. They all wore the color orange and they had strange pointed hats. Ken groaned inwardly. When they all circled the fire chanting a song and holding up sticks, Ken thought that he'd scream. He'd seen enough. He was enraged that some more troublemakers were in the community and more chaos would most probably come from their activities. He hastened away and was able to get home in time for a quick lunch.

Who should he tell about this latest discovery? People were weary of anything out of the ordinary. They had tried to get on with their lives and forget the past craziness. Should he keep this under 'his hat' or tell someone in authority. The new Mayor wasn't going to put up with any more disturbances. Ken decided that he'd wait until the new year and then talk to the Mayor about what he had seen. He hoped that he wouldn't have to report anything. It would be so wonderful if those people just left the mountain never to return.

Star arrived that evening and Ken visited with her for a while at her mother's place. Her mother had disbanded her group and she was working in a local store. She too seemed to want to move on and never discussed what had happened to cause the dissolution of the group. Star was getting on well with her mother. Star talked about all her new friends and activities with great animation. Ken was a little envious to hear that she was having so much fun. His life seemed to be dull in comparison with her new life in the city. He found it hard to talk to her as she had changed from a somewhat shy girl into a confident young woman with many new interests. She promised to come to Ken's place for supper on Christmas day.

Ken had everything ready for Star's arrival. Sure enough she arrived right on time. She was all smiles and she held a big wrapped present. As soon as they got into the house, Star insisted that Ken open the gift. Ken carefully picked away at the present until it was finally unwrapped. It was a compass. It was in a small box at the bottom of the huge box. It was the latest in compasses. He was quite impressed. He thanked Star and then he rushed to get her present which was under the little tree he had found in the forest and which he had decorated carefully. She was excited as she tore open the present and found a pressed flower picture which he had made all himself. The flowers were from the garden of course. She was really pleased with it and admired it for a while and then she gave Ken a hug. They had a great time over the Christmas dinner Ken had prepared. Star kept talking about her experiences at the University and all her new friends. Ken couldn't help but notice that she kept mentioning one boy's name quite a lot. His name was Rob. Ken wondered how close they were but he didn't want to ask Star about him. He was afraid of the answer. He pushed that out of his mind.

The next day Star and Ken went up the mountain to investigate the camp. Ken had told her about what he had seen. It was cold and there was no smoke. Ken hoped that they'd get into the area to investigate further with no one around. Sure enough, there was not a soul to be found. There were only remains of the campfires that had burned there over the past several weeks. They searched for clues as to what had been going on in that area. Some orange clothes and remnants of food were found scattered around in the snow. Ken stumbled over a pyramid-shaped object covered in fake gold. It was sitting on a small table. He wondered why the people had left it there as it probably meant something of significance to them. Then the thought occurred to him that they'd surely come back as this might be a symbol of their beliefs. He started to wipe away the snow in the area around this object and he found a few more of them but they were smaller in size. What had being going on here?

The final clue that cinched it for Ken was when he found a homemade pharaoh's headpiece. This group was most probably somehow connected to ancient Egyptian beliefs! Ken thought he had seen and heard it all but this took the cake. Star said that she thought Ken was on the right track. These people would surely be coming back as this was their place of worship! The strangest of all sights they saw that day was a pyramid shaped building in the trees constructed crudely out of plywood. It was quite large and it was hard to believe that they could have erected it there in the woods. However, they had found an open area and had set it up. The two adventurers entered into the building and found chairs and tables and a raised platform at one end. This was their meeting place. Ken was astonished at what he had seen. Star too, just gazed around in wonder and she was getting somewhat anxious. She wanted to leave as she thought that the people might be coming back. They were both quite chilled and so they hurried like rabbits down the mountain and scurried back to Ken's place to have some hot cocoa and peanut butter cookies (Ken's specialty).

Ken and Star mused over what they had seen that day. Who should they tell about this? Ken said that he was definitely going to inform the Mayor. Star wondered where these people were now. Ken thought that they were probably squatting in the empty houses in town. They both agreed to meet the next day at the section of the town where there were two streets of empty homes. The houses had all been boarded up but Ken and Star were suspicious about whether these homes were really empty. The two friends were apprehensive about what they might find in those homes.

About nine the next morning the two friends crept along behind snow banks at the end of the closed off section of the town. There before them were two rows of homes. They were not greatly surprised to see smoke coming from some of the chimneys! They decided to approach the nearest home by keeping low and slowly inching their way towards the back yard. Sure enough, there before them was evidence of many people dwelling in the home. Many tracks led to the back door. Even though it was still boarded up they could tell by equipment, vehicles and sleds that were carelessly parked everywhere that activity was going on inside.

Ever so slowly the two "detectives" advanced toward the back entrance. Star put her ear to the wall and reported with hand signals that she could hear voices. The two of them suddenly ran to the corner of the building when they heard the back door open. They flattened themselves against the wall and tried to listen to what was happening. It sounded like two men talking about getting supplies from another nearby town. How were they going to get out of Wonder when this section of the town was closed off? This is what was going on in Ken's mind as he listened to the list of supplies that were going to be purchased. All was made clear when the man started up a skidoo with a sled attached to it. Away the man roared over the snow banks and down the road. They could hear the engine roar as it easily ascended the mound of snow at the end of the street. Just before the door closed the two listeners could hear many voices raised in conversation.

Ken and Star stared at one another. Here we go again, thought Ken. This was the perfect place for these "invaders" to hide as no one lived near this section of the town. Just as they were about to explore the next home the door opened again and several children ran outside to play. A woman was watching them carefully. They were not allowed to leave the area. The two spies were able to get to the next home and hide behind some fir trees. From this vantage point they witnessed many people coming in and out of homes. It looked as if they were celebrating something or they might be having "meetings". Who were these people? Where did they come from? Why had no one noticed them? These were the questions that occurred to the onlookers as they witnessed yet another invasion of kooks. The mountains had become restricted zones since the last tragedy. Big signs had been erected. Only local government and forestry officials were allowed on the mountains. However, Ken and Star had been able to get up the mountain quite easily. Security was certainly needed!

The spies had seen enough. They each went their separate ways and agreed to meet the next day for lunch at Ken's place. Star would soon be going back to the city. Ken surmised that she had found Wonder to be a disappointment after the big city lights. The only excitement had been the discovery of this new group. Ken phoned the Mayor's Office and set up an appointment with the Mayor. He wanted to see him as soon as possible before big trouble occurred. He would meet with him in two days. As he gazed up toward White Mountain he wondered what the attraction the mountain held for these people. How did they know about this mountain? Why did these mountains near Wonder attract such strange people? The two mountains looked foreboding as Ken stared at them from his window. Clouds shrouded the peaks and the sun went down behind them causing them to look dark, cold and menacing.

Star came the next day for lunch at Ken's place. They had veggie burgers and potato salad. She told Ken that he was the greatest chef. Ken blushed and offered her a chocolate cookie. He had baked several dozen of them and he gave her a box of them to take back to the city. Star was glad that Ken was going to meet with the Mayor. She had not told her Mother about their discoveries as it would have made her very upset. It would take a long time for her to heal from the past events. Ken and Star agreed that the town didn't need a repeat of all that turmoil again. Ken sadly said good-bye to Star. They hugged and then she was gone. Ken was very despondent for the rest of the day. Star meant a lot to him but he wasn't sure how she felt about him. She had such plans for her future and Ken didn't know if there was room for him in them. They had never had a serious discussion about their feelings for one another. They were just pals or were they? Ken didn't know how he felt about this relationship. However, he sure did miss her!

Frank had been ill for a long time and sadly he was failing fast. Ken visited him the day before he was going to meet with the Mayor. Frank thought that it was a good idea to get the community officials involved as soon as possible. He mumbled about false worship on mountains, which Ken did not understand. Frank was very peaceful about his own end. He said that he knew where he was going. Ken didn't understand about where he could be going to but he didn't want to talk too long with him as he was quite weak. Frank smiled at him as Ken left the room. Ken was sad that his old friend wouldn't be around much longer. Frank had been a father to him. Why did things have to change? Ken wondered about loss and change as he walked back to his home through the crunchy snow. He concluded that he didn't like change very much except if it was for the better and quite often that didn't seem to occur.

Ken marshaled his thoughts as he waited outside the Mayor's office. The Mayor was having a meeting and it was going overtime. Finally, it was Ken's turn to talk to the Mayor. As Ken told him about what he had seen on the mountain the Mayor's eyes widened and a look of horror came to his face and stayed there until Ken had finished. He jumped out of his chair and yelled about crazy people actually living in the closed off area of the town. He grabbed his phone and barked orders right and left and then rushed out of the office. Ken was left staring at the place where the Mayor had been just seconds before he had flashed into action.

The Mayor had rounded up his entire police force which only consisted of five men and they went to the closed off section of the town. When they got there no one would answer and so a siege of sorts began and lasted all that day. The next day the Mayor went with reinforcements from other nearby towns and each home was surrounded by men. Finally, after another day, signs of surrender seemed to be evident. However, when the men approached nearer to the homes, handmade explosives were hurled at them and some were badly hurt. The Mayor had no choice but to get the army involved and two trucks filled with soldiers from the nearest army base arrived just in time. The people finally surrendered on the fourth day. What was not known to the authorities was that several families had not been rounded up as they had gone away to get supplies.

These people had come from Monza in order to practice their Egyptian cultic beliefs. The Mayor was pleased to have nipped this cult in the bud. The whole group (at least the part he had in captivity) were sent packing. They had one hour to collect their belongings and then they were never return to Wonder. Several ring leaders were to be tried for their part in the "bombings". No one realized that this was a determined group that saw White Mountain as their "promised land" and an eviction wasn't going to stop them practicing their rites. A large group of Wonder's citizens witnessed the group leave. A long line of vehicles snaked away down the highway towards Monza. The Mayor smiled broadly at everyone and Ken was hailed as a hero for reporting on these people. Everyone cheered for him and he was carried on the shoulders of some of the young men of the town in a victory ride. Ken was embarrassed about all of this and politely thanked everyone and warned them to keep their eyes on the mountains for any unusual activities. He also was able to get the Mayor to hire security guards to patrol the base of White Mountain.

The new year promised to be a peaceful one or least that was what everyone hoped for as the last few years had been so stressful. Ken spent more time with Frank and his friends in the apartments. That winter was especially cold and so more time was spent inside. No strange activities seemed to be going on in Wonder or on White Mountain. Only people with special permits could ascend it. Ken was learning to paint and he had tried to draw the mountains. He had finished one painting which he thought was quite acceptable. Everyone who saw his work commented on his artistic talent. He even gave one of his pictures to the local little art gallery in Wonder. It was bought several days later! Ken wondered if he could make some money with his artwork.

In March Ken was painting a picture of White Mountain one afternoon and he was looking out of his window at it when he noticed a fire roaring on the south side. What was going on? This must be something freakish because how could a fire burn so vehemently in late winter? The snow had almost gone and old timers predicted that spring had already arrived. It was drier and hotter than was usual for that time of year. Had there been a lightning strike? He had heard thunder during the night. Sometimes lightning struck in winter but that didn't happen too often. Was someone playing with explosives? He phoned the emergency line (which had been set up for the reporting of unusual events). When he got to the mountain the firemen were already there but they were unsure as to how to attack the fire which was raging out of control by this time. It was so far up the mountain that a plane would have to be used to put it out. Some men were already up on the mountain trying their best to stop it but it was a losing battle. More reinforcements were coming but they were needed now. Ken asked if anyone had reported anything unusual before the fire was noticed. Sure enough, someone in Wonder had reported that several vans had been seen going towards the mountain. They were unusually colored and decorated vans. Ken felt like someone had punched him.

All day the firemen and reinforcements battled the fire. Fortunately two planes had been used to douse the fire. Everyone was exhausted but relieved that the fire had not spread and that it was finally out. Firefighters did not find anything suspicious but a wide area had been totally burned out and if there had been evidence it was gone. The Mayor called for a town meeting the next day. Ken was fatigued as he had been helping out all that day and he dragged himself to his little home. His cats meowed to be fed and he stumbled around trying to feed them and he fell exhausted on his couch. Ken had dreams about "Egyptians" dancing around a pyramid which was set on fire and explosives were used to add an "effect". The "Egyptians" ran for their lives and everything was destroyed. Ken often had crazy dreams after he had been involved in intense situations.

The meeting the next day was a solemn one as everyone was afraid that the "Egyptian" group was back again. Several people stood up to report strange things that they had witnessed. Strangers had been seen around the town. They didn't appear to be tourists or visitors. Some men bought a lot of supplies from the hardware store. Strange vehicles had been seen. Smoke had been reported a few times on the mountain. Investigations had not revealed anything. The Mayor reminded everyone to be vigilant. Several patrols would check out the mountain twice a day for the next few months. There was a sign up sheet for those who wanted to volunteer. Although Ken was weary of it all he felt it was his duty to help out in this situation. The town could have been burned. Things could turn ugly again.

What no one realized was that there was an entrance to the mountain on the north side which had not been used until now. The south side of the mountain faced Wonder. On the north side there were no towns but there was a highway which ran by it. The patrols and security men were always on the south side of the mountain. No one had thought to go around the mountain or over it to the other side. No one knew that an even larger group of people had great plans for the north side of the mountain. They were disaffected intellectuals from Monza who had concocted a religion that believed that the north side of White Mountain was sacred. They had sold all that they had and pooled their considerable resources to start a colony on the mountain. They were going to await the end of the Earth and the beginning of the dawn of a new civilization. They had started out on the south side of the mountain to fool everyone. Wonder would witness trouble like never before and they were little prepared for what was going to take place. This group was driven by stubborn, visionary energy.

Chapter Ten
Pelicans in the Wilderness

It was well into April and all seemed quiet and normal in Wonder. Spring had definitely come as had been predicted by long time citizens of the area. There was no snow and the wind was blowing warm and sometimes hot breezes. Ken was pleased to see the beginnings of buds on trees and he gazed at his growing garden and blooming flowers. One Saturday Ken decided to go for a hike. He took his walking stick and a packsack and headed out looking around to see how everything was growing in the forest. He saw some indications of wildlife scurrying around and birds chirping happily. He saw a brown rabbit bounce away from him. Ken took in a long breath of fresh air and dreamed about the time when he could own some land and call it his very own. He had tried to save as much as he could over the last few years but it wasn't enough for the land he had in mind. It was a five acre parcel of land closer to White Mountain and about ten miles from town. It had a nice home on it and there were lots of trees and a small river ran through the property. He decided to walk to that area and look at it again as he had many times before. The home was being rented as the owner was living in Monza. Ken sat on a little hill looking at the idyllic setting. He imagined what he would do with the land. As he sat there in the sun, munching a sandwich and dreaming happy thoughts, he was startled from his revere by an approaching bus which was heading down the road towards the house. The bus stopped at the house! Out piled about twenty people! They all seemed to be young adults. Animated conversations and whoops of joy assailed Ken's ears. The door to the home opened and several other young adults hailed the newcomers with cheers and hugs and back slaps. Ken almost fell over when he thought that he saw Star! It couldn't be her! He decided that he had to get a lot closer and find out what was going on and if Star was really there. He knew that the University was on a break and perhaps it was her! Why didn't she contact him? Ken had wild thoughts as he inched toward the house. He hadn't heard from her for a while. Perhaps she had decided that their friendship was no more and that she had decided to stick with her University friends and forget all about him.

Ken was able to get close enough to the back door to take a quick peek through a small window in it. What he saw horrified him. Everyone was yelling and shouting and laughing all at the same time and the place seemed to be almost destroyed! People were being pushed and some were play fighting. They were a rowdy crowd! Then Ken saw Star! She was hugging a tall dark haired young man! Ken felt sick. He scurried away determined to let the owner know that his place was being almost demolished. He didn't care if Star got caught! He was so hurt about what he had seen and his heart felt like a stone. He trudged through melting snow stabbing the ground with his walking stick. Even the sight of an elk didn't phase him as he angrily pushed on towards Wonder. He went straight to his phone when he got home. Fortunately, he was able to get the owner right away. He informed him of all that he had seen and the owner thanked him. The owner was Randy Armitage who owned many properties. Randy said that he would investigate this matter that very day. He would fly his plane to a nearby airport. Ken offered to meet him at the airport and drive him to him to the property. Randy agreed that they'd meet at the airport about four that afternoon.

At the appointed time Ken was at the airport and he watched as a small plane landed and then taxied and came to a stop in front of the small terminal. Ken smiled at the busy businessman as they shook hands. He said that he'd have to park his plane in the hanger. Ken took Randy's bag and they agreed to meet in the terminal. After the plane was put into the hanger, Randy and Ken had a quick bite in the little restaurant in the terminal. Ken filled in Randy about all the details. The two of them set off for the property and after about half an hour they arrived at the house. It was dark and all the lights were on in the house. As they got out of the car they could tell that high reveling was taking place. The air was filled with the strangest music that Ken had ever heard. The pulsating beat was matched by the gyrating bodies that could be seen through the front window. Randy was livid! He pounded on the front door and finally it was opened by a jovial fellow with a pyramid hat on his head! Obviously he didn't know who Randy was and he invited them in with a flourish of his hand. Ken was almost afraid to look at the crowd of intoxicated people. His eyes met Star's and she blushed. Everyone was dressed like Egyptian royalty with headdresses. Star looked like an Egyptian princess. The place had been totally wrecked!

Randy cornered the two renters and informed them that they had half an hour to get their things together and get out. All the rest of them were ordered out. Finally after the last reveler had left, including Star who didn't look at Ken as she left, Randy and Ken surveyed the damage. The whole house would have to be gutted! It looked as it someone had gone crazy! In the middle of one of the bedrooms they found a big pyramid made from cardboard. There were cat symbols and smaller pyramids everywhere. Ken realized that this was the same group (or some more members of it) that had been on White Mountain. White Mountain wasn't too far away. The walls had been kicked in and some destroyed to make one big room downstairs. There was old food and garbage all over the house. Randy and Ken decided to stay the night in case anyone returned. It was creepy trying to get some sleep in that spooky house. Ken wrapped himself in a curtain that had been torn off the window by the invaders. Randy found a blanket and tried to clear away a space in order to lie down. Finally, about midnight they both fell into a fitful sleep. In his dreams Ken saw Star smiling at him and then disappearing into a mist. The weird music kept replaying in his dreams.

After a long discussion, Ken and Randy came to an agreement. Randy asked if Ken could keep a watch out on the property for him. He was going to have the whole house fixed up and then Ken could rent it if he wanted to and hopefully, some day be able to buy it from Randy. Ken was overjoyed! He readily agreed to come to the property several times a week until the workmen could come to do the renovations. He was very upset with Star but he tried to focus on this new opportunity. He would check on the property three times a week.

On the first visit Ken found nothing out of order. Everything was as they had left it. On the second visit Ken noticed that the front door was open. He was sure that he had locked it. On entering the house he noticed that there were signs that someone had been there. Some of the furniture had been changed around as if to provide a place to sleep. Carefully, Ken surveyed the rest of the house. Some half eaten food and open cans were on the kitchen counter. After checking out the entire house he found the entrance point. A back window had been smashed and that had allowed the culprit or culprits to enter the house. Whoever or whomever had been there had gone. Perhaps it was only vagrants and not the University crowd. Ken hurried back to town and phoned Randy right away. Randy was very upset and asked Ken to board up all the windows. Ken got the supplies he needed and headed for the house in his truck which he had recently bought from the ailing Frank.

Ken was very tired after he had boarded up the house. He sat down in the kitchen to eat a sandwich and to drink some juice that he had brought along with him. He heard some rustling at the back of the house and he peered through a small knothole in one of the boarded windows. Two scruffy-looking men were walking around trying to peer into the house without success. Then they were at the front door. Fortunately Ken had locked the door. There was a lot of pounding and banging and kicking on the door. Finally, it seemed as if the men had left. Slowly, Ken cracked open the front door. The two men were snooping around his truck. Ken was glad that he had locked it securely. After a while, the men stumbled off into the brush. Ken's heart was pounding! How was he, alone, going to keep this property secure?

Ken went back to his place and phoned Randy again and gave him the latest information. Randy decided that he'd step up the repairs and have a crew there at the house the next day. The crew would also live there until the job was completed. Ken was relieved and thought that this was a great solution. He went to visit Frank who was not doing well and would soon pass away. He had preferred to die in his own bed. He told Ken that he knew where he was going and that it was going to be a glorious homecoming. Ken didn't quite understand what he meant but he didn't want to tire Frank out with questions. He knew that Frank had a peace that he didn't have and he also knew that Frank was a God-fearing man who was loved by all who knew him. When Ken mentioned a few facts about what had been going on in and around the house, Frank murmured something about pelicans in the wilderness. He was trying to explain that these people were doomed to failure. Then he softly said that the Egyptians were men and that they weren't God. Ken was puzzled. However, he felt assured that all this craziness would end and that these people would not bother them again. Even though Frank wouldn't last the night, Ken was at peace. All would be well, in the end.

The next day was a Sunday and the residents of the apartments gathered together to mourn the passing of Frank who had passed away very early that morning. Ken stood with them as they all gathered in the garden. They sang some hymns and some said prayers and some spoke kindly about their beloved friend and leader. Frank was buried three days later in the middle of the garden. The rose arbour would bloom in the summer above the grave. There were a lot of tears that day. Ken cried too. His 'father' had gone away and he would not return.

Chapter Eleven
Locusts Among Us

A few weeks later the reading of Frank's will took place in his lawyer's office in Wonder. Friends, family members and Ken were present. He had been asked to attend and he had been surprised. There were about twenty people there that day. Some of the people from the apartments were there too. After the family had heard what Frank had left them, Ken's name was mentioned. He sat up because he was surprised to hear his name. Frank had left Ken both apartment buildings! He also had left a few personal items. Ken couldn't believe his ears! Everyone was looking at him. Some family members had looks of great puzzlement on their faces. They did not know who Ken was and they peered at him intently. Shortly after the reading of the will a number of family members talked with Ken about his relationship with Frank. Ken could tell that they were as amazed by all of this as he was and he felt uncomfortable talking to them.

It took quite a while for Ken to realize that he was the sole owner of the apartment buildings. The tenants all seemed pleased to have Ken as their landlord. He would receive all their rent payments. This sudden influx of cash was a great change. He had to consider what he would do with this sudden wealth. He still wanted to live in Randy's house. The thought struck him that he would be able to buy it! He rushed to phone Randy. He was really happy to hear Ken's news and he arranged to meet with Ken as soon as possible to finalize the sale of the house. Ken would now be responsible for paying for and overseeing the renovations on the house. The house price was reduced due to all the damage it had incurred.

A few weeks later the house was Ken's. The renovations were nearly complete and Ken would move in the following week. Spring was definitely showing itself. There was very little snow and trees and shrubs had leaves. There had not been any further suspicious activities either on the mountain or around Ken's new property. Ken had hired a middle-aged man to take over his job. He was one of the former Blue Group men. He would live in Ken's little house that had been such a cozy home for these past years. He wouldn't have to pay rent. Ken was happy to know who would now live in that little abode. Everything was turning out so well.

However "locusts" were destroying the land. There were not literal locusts but there were people on the mountain carving out an empire for themselves. The north side was being changed! They were careful not to use fire and they worked a lot at night. They felt that they were safe from all eyes. They were wrong. Ellie Welsh lived on the edge of Wonder and she had noticed something out of order one day. A big truck roared past her place and headed around the side of White Mountain. There had never been a road around that side of the mountain. It was more like a trail. She decided to investigate. She was a retired school teacher who had time to check this matter out to her satisfaction. She was fit and fifty-five and she liked to hike.

One morning in April she set out to have a look at that trail or road. To her surprise she found that the trail had been widened and brush had been cut and tire tracks were clearly visible. It had been turned into a road! She ducked just in time as she heard the throbbing engine of a truck coming towards her from the other side of the mountain. From her vantage point she could see clearly into the truck as it roared by at top speed. About five young men were in it and they all seemed to be having a great time. The truck box was empty. Ellie mused that they were probably going for supplies. As Ellie loved mysteries and solving them, she decided to play detective.

At home she packed some food, water, a blanket and warm clothing. She planned to follow that road and find out what was at the other end of it. She was excited at the thought of solving this puzzle. Ellie didn't think that she'd need any backup help because she was an independent soul and did things her way. As a long time resident of Wonder she felt that it was her obligation to get to the bottom of what was happening on the other side of the mountain. She did not abide fools very well and the past history of groups in the village (which had recently become a town) had been very upsetting. Perhaps she could nip this in the bud. If this was yet another group, she'd know about it and broadcast the information far and wide!

Ellie set out on foot up the dusty road which really looked somewhat like a widened trail. The day was bright and dry and Ellie hummed to herself as she trudged along the road and began to go around the side of White Mountain. She didn't meet any trucks or cars or people. All was still as if waiting for something to occur.

Around noon she stopped to eat some of her food by the side of the road. She hid herself in some bushes just in case somebody came down the road. After taking a short rest, Ellie set out again on her quest. She had begun to climb higher along the road. The road was leading upwards instead of around the mountain. Ellie had to take more rest stops. As she was getting her breath she heard the sound of vehicles coming toward her. She ducked into the brush and sat very still like a frightened rabbit. Sure enough two trucks emerged from around the corner full of people. Ellie was able to count about twenty young-looking people. They were all in good spirits. Where were they heading? Surely they wouldn't go into Wonder. She had noticed what looked like luggage and then she thought that they were heading back down the mountain to where they had come from originally.

After the noise of the trucks had died down, Ellie continued on her climb. She felt that she should be near the top of the mountain. It was about four o'clock when she reached what appeared to be an encampment. She took her bearings with a compass that she'd brought along with her and she found out that she was now on the northwest side of the mountain. The top of the mountain could be seen and it didn't seem to be that far away. The encampment appeared to have been deserted. There were a few small buildings and a supply of lumber and tools. Ellie didn't want to investigate the buildings as she felt as if someone was watching her from somewhere nearby. What should she do? She wanted evidence.

After watching from afar for about fifteen minutes and not hearing or seeing anyone, she stepped forward towards the nearest building. As she neared it a man stepped out of its doorway! Another man followed. They ran at her and grabbed her so fast that she didn't have time to scream. Quickly they pushed her into the building. They tied her hands and feet and tied a dirty handkerchief over her mouth. Ellie was in a state of sheer terror and panic! What was going to happen to her?

The two men sat looking at her and warning her that she was not to try to escape. They were young men in their early twenties. It was now dark and the two men ate some cold beans and bread. They let Ellie eat some of her own food that was in her packsack. They had looked through it carefully before allowing her to get food from it. They took the handkerchief from her mouth. While Ellie was eating she ventured to ask them who they were and why they were keeping her against her will. They didn't tell her anything but warned her that she better not scream or the handkerchief would be tied over her mouth again. Ellie knew that they meant business and she resigned herself to the fact that she wouldn't be going back to her home that night. She asked if she could go to relieve herself. One of the men led her to a makeshift biffy and stood outside it. Ellie was so humiliated. Why hadn't she told anyone where she was going? She had been a fool to come on her own.

The taller of the two men showed her where to sleep for the night. Thankfully, he did not put the handkerchief over her mouth. She used her blanket for her "bed". She rolled up her jacket to use as a pillow. They were going to sleep on the other side of the building. Somehow she fell into a fitful sleep in which mountains exploded and people ran screaming. When she woke up, sunlight streamed through the open door. The men were gone. Slowly Ellie sat up and she noticed that she had been untied! Carefully she made her way to the door. No one appeared to around. This was too good to be true. Was she going to be able to get away from those men? Quickly she grabbed her packsack and pushed everything into it. She decided to make a run for it. Far off up the mountain she heard some hammering. Maybe the men were constructing something and they thought she wouldn't try to leave. As Ellie ran with every ounce of energy she could muster, one of the young men emerged from the trees and shouted at her to stop at once. Of course Ellie wasn't going to stop and she was able, somehow, to head deep into the forest. The sound of breaking branches and running feet kept her from stopping. The man was running towards her!

She decided to take a zigzag course. After a while she didn't hear anything. However, she was totally lost! Where was the road? Where was she? She imagined bears walking towards her and every little noise and breeze made her jump. She got out her compass and looked around for moss on the north side of trees. She needed to go southeast. After getting her bearings, she set forth to find the road home. An hour passed by and finally she began to see that she was heading towards the road! As she stepped onto the road she realized that she had come quite far down the mountain and that she was not that far from Wonder. It only took her an hour to get home. She was so relieved and happy that she sat in her kitchen and wept. A little later as she sat in her bathtub soaking her sore, tired and filthy body, she wondered who she should tell about what she had witnessed.

Ellie phoned the Mayor and told him everything. He thanked her for her call and told her to take care of herself. As she looked out of her window she wondered when that road would be packed with vehicles from Wonder. She didn't have long to wait. A long cavalcade of police cars, vans and trucks filled with men raced up the dusty road. Ellie could only imagine what would take place at the campsite. That evening she saw the same vehicles coming slowly down the road. What had happened? After about half an hour her phone rang and it was the Mayor. He told her that they hadn't found anyone on the mountain and that the campsite had been demolished! They didn't go further up the mountain but they planned to go up there the next day. He warned her not to go up there again. Ellie assured him that she'd never go anywhere near that road!

Ken was asked to join the posse to investigate the northeast side of White Mountain. He had been horrified to learn about Ellie's misadventures on the mountain. He knew her and liked her and he hoped that she was all right. Imagine kidnapping an older lady! Ken was amazed that this road had been constructed under everyone's noses. As he headed around and up the mountain in his truck with several other men from the apartments, he wondered what they would find. All of the vehicles stopped at the point of entrance to the demolished campsite. As they sifted through the wreckage, they found strange objects and pyramid shaped boxes. Ken was angry at the thought of the 'Egyptians' still on the mountain. Then the whole group headed up the mountain looking for the other construction site. They found it and were amazed at what was there among the tall fir trees.

Rising from the forest floor was a huge pyramid-shaped building. It had several steps up to it. It was constructed out of plywood and logs from the forest. Upon further investigation, another road was found leading away from it down on the north side of the mountain. There were thus, two ways to get to it. The double doors were locked with big bolts. There were no windows. It was decided that they wouldn't force an entrance but would wait a few days and return to see if anyone was there. Ken wondered if Star would return. The University break was over and therefore the students wouldn't be back for a while. Ken was sure that this group was composed of University students. Ellie had only seen young people. Ken shared his thoughts with the Mayor and it was agreed that only Ken and a few others would come back to check on this site over the next few weeks. The locusts had been very busy on that mountain!

Chapter Twelve
Foxes in the Desert

Ken and two men visited the site three times over the next month and no activity was noticed. The students had drawn strange pictures all over the pyramid building. Perhaps they hoped to paint them in different colors. It was boring, tedious work going up and down the mountain but they all felt that it was their civic duty. It was now the end of May. The students might return for "summer work". Teams of men from Wonder were ready to take shifts on the mountain. This time they wouldn't let these intruders disappear. Ken was enjoying his new home. He had a dog now and she was a like a guard dog but she had a gentle nature. Ken had named her Oregano but he called her Oree. Slowly he had got over his great disappointment in Star and he was looking forward to a bright future. His new home was perfect. However, "foxes" were surrounding the whole community area and they were on the hunt.

One of the mountain shifts noticed activity at the beginning of June. They had spied on several young men hiking up White Mountain with large knapsacks. They followed them to the site of the giant pyramid. They watched them start to paint the designs and pictures on the oddly-shaped building. They also started to create a larger clearing by attacking the trees with axes. The mountain shift reported this to the Mayor and he notified the Forestry Department. Several forest rangers along with some policemen all ascended the mountain to order the intruders off the mountain once and for all. When they got there no one was to be found. The rangers and the policemen set about destroying the building. After all it was illegal to dwell on or build on the mountain. It was Government property as well as part of a National Park Reserve. It was also a restricted zone due to all the problems that there had been on it. As they were demolishing the building they noticed smoke further down the mountain. They all rushed down the mountain to discover a roaring fire making its way toward them. They were fortunate to be able to escape and they sent a fire crew to put it out. These students were dangerous!

The destruction of the pyramid was completed the next day and all thought that surely this would be the end of activity on the mountain. The mountain shifts were curtailed. Everyone was enjoying a wonderful summer and few gave any thoughts about anything more than their holiday plans or how well their gardens were growing. Ken had planted a large garden full of all kinds of vegetables. He worked in it often and enjoyed watching the progress of each plant. He also had created wonderful landscapes of different kinds of flowers and shrubs all around his house. He was also building a large deck behind the house so that he could sit on it and view everything. Oree loved to chase balls and so she kept Ken busy throwing balls and bringing them back to him and so he had to throw them again and again. Ken planned to have a picnic at his place for all of the apartment residents. Fifty people would be able to come and enjoy a fun filled afternoon at his place. It was only three days away and Ken was busy arranging who would bring what and how he was going to accommodate such a huge crowd.

To Ken's surprise Star was back in town. Although she had not contacted Ken he knew from the reports of local busybodies that she was back for a short visit. He did not want to have anything to do with her and he would try not to run into her if he could help it. One day in the Post Office he saw her buying stamps. She did not acknowledge his presence and she stared right through him. Ken was glad that he didn't have to speak to her. He was somewhat taken aback by the coldness in her eyes. She looked so different. He couldn't quite put his finger on what had changed in her demeanor but she definitely wasn't the Star he had known. She walked right by him and she headed toward the main entrance of the Post Office. Ken left the Post Office shortly after that and he saw her walking down the sidewalk with the tall young man he had seen her with at his home. He knew that she was not his friend anymore. He hoped that the group wasn't somewhere nearby planning yet another assault on the mountain. He pushed that thought out of his mind and went about gathering supplies for his picnic.

Everyone showed up for the picnic. Even the oldest resident was there in a wheelchair. Oree was having great fun running after balls. The cats were enjoying being fussed over and being fed tidbits. There was tons of food and everyone loved Ken's special dessert that he had created which he called Chocolate Mint Bars. They went fast. The laughter and fun lasted well into the evening and the last guest left about nine o'clock. Several ladies had cleaned up everything and so Ken had little to do but stack the chairs and load them into his truck to take back to the apartments the next day. Everyone agreed that this should be an annual event. As Ken was locking up for the night he thought that he heard some noise in the forest that faced his property. He turned off his lights and looked out of his front window. He saw a campfire and people huddled around it. Ken felt a great sinking feeling in the pit of his stomach. He knew that THEY were back!

When the campfire burned down to its last ember, the campers lay around it in what looked like sleeping bags. Ken kept watch until he was too tired to keep his eyes open. After a restless night he awoke later than usual and found out that it was ten o'clock already. He raced to the front window but he saw nothing at all. They were gone. Carefully he made his way towards the campfire. He found burnt cigarettes, beer bottles and garbage. He hoped against hope that they would not come back again. Were they spying on him? He cleared the area and reported the illegal campfire to the local forest ranger. He said that he would patrol the area.

The "campers" didn't return and so Ken relaxed. Life went on as usual. It was August and there was a hint of autumn days to come in the deep blue sky. Ken was harvesting his garden and freezing and canning all kinds of vegetables. He went into town a few times a week to check on his apartments and to talk to his maintenance man, Ben. Ben was enjoying his job and his little house and he, too had two cats which he had named Foosie and Tawny. There appeared to be no trouble and all was peaceful and pure contentment. It seemed that way. Ken looked up at the deep blue sky and he knew that winter would be coming all too soon. He saw several flocks of geese fly overhead toward the south. Way up high eagles screamed and dove and then rose to fly higher and higher. Ken could see the tops of White Mountain and Black Mountain. There was no sign of smoke. They just stood there solid and mysterious as ever.

Ken was busy canning one evening in early September when he heard what sounded like a truck coming down the road past his house. It was headed toward Wonder. He stepped to the window and to his surprise it was full of young people standing or sitting in the back. Ken felt instantly sick to his stomach. **They** were back! Why were they coming back at all and why now? He decided to call the Mayor at his home right away. The Mayor was not at home but he left a message. He then called the Head of the Town Council. He too, was not at home. Ken thought that they must all be at a meeting. He called the local police detachment and they promised to keep a look out for them. Ken worried that somehow the truck would give everyone the slip and then what would these young people do next? About an hour later a police officer called Ken to inform him that the truck had not been seen but that road blocks had been set up. The local detachment would continue to keep a lookout for them.

Ken went into town the next day and informed the Mayor of the developments. He was upset that trouble might yet again be brewing. The only problem was that the truck had not been spotted. Ken decided to investigate. He called in on Ellie to tell her to stay put as there may be trouble in her area. She offered Ken some cake and coffee and then gave him a thermos of hot tea to take with him on his search. Ken set out just before noon. There were clouds in the sky and rain had been forecasted. The weather had been cooler than normal and everyone thought an early winter would be coming soon. Ken had brought a raincoat and he was wearing sturdy boots. He went along the edge of the road that Ellie had traveled and he met no one. However, he did notice that there were tire tracks. A truck had gone up this road! The tracks looked fresh.

He very cautiously picked his way along the side of the road until he reached the place where it ended. Now he was on the north side, having traveled upward and around the side of the mountain. He was able to duck out of sight when he noticed activity ahead. It looked like a crew was trying to extend the road to reach the top of the mountain! Bushes and trees were being destroyed and men worked shoveling gravel and smoothing it down. Of course this road building was illegal. There were two trucks. One was a gravel truck and the other held equipment. It was the one Ken had seen go by his house. Some girls were there too. They were working hard too and then all the activity stopped and everyone took a break. It was getting on in the afternoon. They all sat by the side of the road sipping coffee and eating doughnuts. They were all in great spirits. Ken felt some raindrops on his hands and nose and then it started to pour. Everyone jumped up and huddled under a tarp in the back of the equipment truck. Ken had seen enough and so he headed back down and around the mountain. He slipped several times and he was covered in mud and miserably cold and wet when he knocked on Ellie's door after about an hour and a half.

Ellie ushered Ken into her warm little kitchen and told him to take off his wet socks and raincoat. She gave him some work socks and soon he was warming up by her fireplace with a cup of cocoa in his hand. When he told her about what he had seen her eyes widened and her mouth opened in total surprise. Ellie said that he could stay at her place overnight so that he could watch the road for the trucks. They would surely be coming down that road. Ken and Ellie closed the front curtains and left slits open so that they could look at the road. Sure enough about an hour later the trucks were heard on the road. Ken quickly called the police station to alert them as to where the trucks were heading. The road led through the town. The truck crews had some different ideas. They pulled up in front of Ellie's house! Ellie almost screamed and Ken checked to see if the doors were locked. All the window curtains had been drawn. Ken and Ellie hoped that the "students" would think that no one was at home. No lights were on in the house. Ken and Ellie had just put out the fire in the fireplace. They kept very still and listened. The two of them heard scuffling sounds by the back door. Someone was trying to pry it open! Ken reached for the phone to inform the police that the students were at Ellie's house and trying to break into it. He told them to hurry.

The sneaky desert foxes planned to use Ellie's house for shelter. They were sure that no one was in it. The biggest man pushed and fiddled with the back doorknob and then three of them ran at the door. Ken and Ellie heard a loud crack as the door split. Ellie felt dizzy and her heart started to race. Ken whispered to her to take deep breaths. Just as the men were about to demolish the door sirens were heard and all the door bashing activity stopped. Everyone took off on foot in all directions. When the police arrived no one was there and several policemen fanned out to try and catch at least some of them. The only one they caught was ... Star! She looked so angry at being caught. She was hustled into a squad car all the while giving Ken glaring stares. Ken was pale and totally drained from all the excitement. Poor Ellie had to have some first aid which was given to her by one of the policewomen. She was now sitting in her favorite chair by the rekindled fire. Her breathing had turned to normal. She begged Ken to stay the night. A policeman also planned to stay on guard.

Not one of the "foxes" was captured. Star was released with warnings about not going up that road again. She had refused to talk about any of the activities that she had been involved in on the mountain. Her Mother had to pay a hefty fine for Star's trespassing in a restricted area. Star and her Mother were again, not on good terms. Star left for the City the next day. Ken could not believe that this was the girl who had been such a great friend. Ken surmised that the students wanted to make the road before the snow flew. He knew nothing about what was really planned for that mountain.

Ken went to town the next day and returned with a new door for Ellie. The police were going to regularly patrol her road for about three weeks. Ellie was still shaken and she didn't want Ken to leave. Ken decided to put her into one of his apartments for a while. He moved some of her things for her and Ellie was quite contented with this arrangement. After living there for several weeks she asked if she could rent the apartment on a permanent basis. She planned to sell her home. Ellie was now one of the Open Arms community. She had already made several friends. She soon fit in with the "baking group". She got the bright idea of setting up a small bakery and Ken got permission from the town to sell baked goods from a small "store" he was going to build on the edge of the apartment property. Her speckled doughnuts were an immediate favorite. The bakers couldn't wait to set up their little bakery. They had decided to call it 'Sweet Treats'. All this happy activity helped ease the pain of the past weeks.

The "students" weren't seen until one day in early November. Ken surmised that they were on a University break. He saw the same truck go by his place. It was a cold, crisp day and snow was forecast for that day. He thought that they were quite brazen to whiz past his place. He decided to follow behind them in his truck from a discreet distance. Sure enough they drove right past Ellie's old place (which had been sold to a young family) and then they headed up the forbidden road. They took down the barriers and proceeded on up the road. Ken was astonished! At the end of the road they all got out and trudged around the mountain and out of sight. Ken had seen enough and he turned around his truck and headed back to Wonder. Snow was beginning to fall quite heavily and Ken wondered how they would get back down the mountain. He decided to wait at Ellie's old home for about an hour to see if they came back. The young family were happy to have his company and when it started to grow dark they invited him to eat supper with them. They too, had moved from Monza to get away from the city. They had a little girl named Molly who looked like a little princess with golden curls. Mary and Matthew Smith told Ken that they were enjoying Wonder and the beautiful setting. Matthew was a nurse in the Wonder Hospital. The Hospital had grown over the years and new staff had been hired recently. As they ate supper, Ken told them about all the strange goings on that had occurred on both mountains over the years. They were amazed at the number of odd groups that had come to the area. He then filled them in on the latest activities. The kitchen table had been moved into the living room so that they could all look out the big window to see if they saw any lights from the truck coming down the road. Nothing was seen on the road in all the time Ken was with the family.

Chapter Thirteen
Poison

Ken finally left the young family about nine o'clock that evening. He had great difficulty getting to his place as the snow had really piled up and it was icy. The plows had not come out yet and so Ken took an extra long time to finally arrive at his house. He was concerned about the students. Where were they? He phoned the Mayor at his home and he told Ken that a search party would set out early the next day. He told Ken that even though these young people were pests, they could have faced some real danger up there on the mountain. Ken was worried too. He thought that he had seen Star with them. He had a very fitful sleep and was up early to join the search party that was going to meet at the Town Hall. Everyone had dressed warmly and rescue equipment and supplies were piled into a town truck. Ken and several men (including some local firefighters) drove behind the supply truck. Several other trucks followed behind Ken.

As they proceeded to the road that led to the mountain they noticed that no new tire marks were evident. The whole area was snowed in and everyone drove very slowly. Fortunately the vehicles all had chains. When they got to the mountain road there was no sign that any vehicle had passed by on it. This did not bode well for the students. They all drove carefully up the road. When they got as far as it was possible, they all got out to trek up the mountain on foot. Finally, they reached the students' truck. They then trudged around the mountain. After an hour they were about mid point on the north side. They heard not a sound. It was deathly silent. Everyone was on edge. What would they find? After milling around in the area they all sat down to have some food and to discuss what to do next. The snow had stopped and all they could hear was the plop of snow falling off tree branches. It was warming up a little and the sun was trying to come out behind the grey clouds that floated above them. They all marveled at the silence. It was decided that they would begin calling out for them in case they needed help. After about half an hour of calling and shouting they had received no replies. Their next plan was to fan out (each with a compass) in a horizontal formation to determine if the students were anywhere near this general area. This plan produced no results except that one man fell and he was now limping. After a brief blast of sun it was now getting darker. It was time to go back to Wonder. They were all discouraged and anxious. What had happened to the students?

Another search party went up the mountain the next day and for several days after that and no one was found. It seemed that the students had vanished into the mountain air. The search parties decided to go down the north side of the mountain and when they were closer to the bottom of it they found that there was evidence left by a large group of people. It seemed like a settlement of sorts. There was a road that connected with the main road that ran beside the mountain. Several huts and fire pits were discovered. This was probably where the students finally got to and then left for the City. The site was promptly destroyed. Everyone thought that this was finally an end to the students' activities on the mountain. They were wrong. A poison was working its way into the whole surrounding area and no one was going to be able to find a quick antidote for its pernicious destruction.

Christmas came and went with festivities and relaxation. Ken had several parties at his place with much merriment had by all who came to feast and to play games. Oree always enjoyed it when people came to the house. The cats hid away in dark corners waiting for the intruders to leave their sanctuary. Echo and Daisy had died and now Ken had two new cats named Jerry and Josephine (Jo Jo). They were brother and sister and they got into mischief together. Ken enjoyed having everyone in his home. They all tried to forget the "goings on" and to look forward to a wonderful new year. Ellie had a New Year's party at her place where they played Monopoly with much shouting and cheering. Matthew and Mary along with Molly came to the party, too. They all enjoyed watching the town's little fireworks display at midnight. Ken was so happy with his life and friends. He had pushed his disappointment over Star into the back of his mind and he hoped that some day he would not remember her with pain.

January was snowy and bitterly cold. Ken spent a lot of time painting and he had produced quite a lot of pictures. He was thinking of going to Monza to see if he could sell some of them in a few galleries. One gallery was interested in him putting on a show of his works. Ken hoped to be able to have enough pieces completed by

March to be able to put on the show. His cats liked to curl up for hours in front of the fireplace. Oree would join them and there would be some jockeying for position. Sometimes Oree would be sleeping in front of the fireplace with the two cats laying on top of her! Ken took a picture of this 'arrangement' one day and planned to paint a picture of it.

One morning in the middle of February Ken noticed a truck parked on the road in front of his house. He had never seen it before and he decided to keep an eye on it. No one seemed to be around. After half an hour of observation, Ken saw a middle-aged man come from across the road and get into the truck and drive away. Ken thought that this was odd. Several hours later it returned and the man was accompanied by several young men and they all went into the forest to the east of Ken's house. They had some poles and orange flags. Where they staking out some property borders? After an hour they returned to the truck and left. Ken went over to investigate. Sure enough there were poles with orange flags and they were set up to mark off a large area. Ken gasped when he saw a Private Property sign. These people had bought some property near to his place! Who were they? Why did they buy it?

Ken went into the only Real Estate agent's office in town. He asked him if someone had bought property near his place. He was informed that yes indeed, a man from Monza had bought three acres to the east of Ken's place. This man was a Professor at the University of Monza. Ken quickly put two and two together and came up with what he thought was happening right before his eyes. The students and their "guru" were going to set up their "Egyptian" settlement near to his place! Ken walked slowly out of the office in a dazed state of mind. He went over to the Town Hall to speak with the Mayor. The Mayor said that he couldn't stop anyone from buying land. Ken was told to report any disturbances. Ken's little, peaceful world was going to be disrupted. He was depressed. He definitely was going to report anything out of the ordinary!

Nothing happened on the land until the beginning of March. Another break from studies brought a load of students who were working hard on building a large oddly-shaped building. The spring was warm and they had been able make a foundation for the building. When the students were gone Ken surveyed the shape of it and he couldn't make out what it was going to be at all. There had been no disturbances other than the sound of hammers and the backhoe digging away into the soil. They even waved at Ken with friendly hellos. After two weeks they were all gone. Ken enjoyed the peace and quiet. Shouldn't these people have been arrested because of their previous activities? They couldn't be arrested apparently because no one could be identified and at present they hadn't broken any laws. Ken found this out when he went and talked to the local police.

One day while Ken was looking through one of his history books he saw The Great Sphinx. He thought about the shape of it and then he looked at it again and gasped. Were they going to build a building in the shape of a sphinx? If so, then why? Ken read up about the sphinx and it apparently was a guardian symbol. What were they going to guard? Ken tried to concentrate on his painting. He was going to go into Monza in a few days to put on his one man show in the Rosewood Art Gallery. He was going to show twenty pieces. The pictures were of: landscapes, flowers and animals. They were a reflection of his life in and around Wonder. He planned to stay only a day there and then head straight back to his cozy home.

Ken sat at the back of the art gallery waiting for people to arrive and to view his paintings. A few people arrived and soon the gallery was filled with curious viewers of his artwork. Ken mingled with them and explained when and how he painted each picture. The mountain pictures were favorites. By noon all his pictures had been sold! Ken couldn't believe it! These people actually paid money for his pictures. They seemed to be starved for pictures of nature and animals. Ken left Monza in a daze. The gallery wanted him to put on another one man show in the summer. As he drove toward Wonder he thought that it was ironic that he would come back to Monza from a small mountain town and do so well. He idly wondered if Star liked art. He really didn't know much about her anymore.

When he got home he noticed that all the activity had stopped at the building site. Whatever the shape of the building, it was likely going to be finished by the summer. Ken tried to put the "neighbors" out of his mind. He wished that they'd never return. He couldn't help wondering about them and of course he knew that it was wishful thinking on his part to think that they would abandon their worksite. He was irked at the Mayor for not insisting that they leave the area. They had cleverly escaped being actually caught doing anything illegal but everyone knew that the group had been involved in all the goings on around and on White Mountain. Only Star had been actually caught. He wondered if she was still in the "Egyptian group". Surely she had learned enough about groups from her experiences in Wonder with her mother and all the other crazies. Ken stared out of his kitchen window as he sipped his coffee and he mused about what would happen during the summer months. He didn't fully realize that the poisonous group had come to stay and it wasn't going to leave. They had big plans.

Chapter Fourteen
Fire from God

April was a wonderful month in Wonder. Ken never tired seeing new life springing up all around him. There had been no new activity "next door" and Ken had enjoyed the peace and quiet. He had two new cats. He had two new kittens which he had named Tiny and Tumble. They were two sisters both similar in appearance. They were black and white each with one eye circled with a white patch. They were very shy and scampered away if visitors appeared. Jerry and Jo Jo tolerated their existence. Oree continued to enjoy greeting visitors and playing games with them. Ken enjoyed playing with his animals on his backyard lawn.

One afternoon in late April Ken was throwing a ball to Oree for about the twentieth time when he heard something. There was a loud voice blaring something from what might be a bullhorn. Ken raced around to the front of his property and witnessed the strangest sight that he had ever seen (and of course he had seen many strange things living in Wonder). A man in a long orange robe and with a long white beard was standing on the road roaring into a bullhorn. He was shouting about wrath and God and hellfire. He looked like he had appeared out of nowhere. He was pointing in the direction of the "Egyptian site". He was promising swift destruction on the entire group and their property. He was ordering them to leave. Ken hesitated but then approached the raving man. He put his hand up as if to show that he was friendly. The man put down his bullhorn and stared straight at Ken with his two dark, beady eyes. Ken told him that the group wasn't there on the site. The man sputtered something about general warnings and then turned and headed down the road towards Wonder. Ken followed him and asked him if he needed lodging or food. The man told Ken that he had his own group of followers waiting for him in Wonder. Ken inwardly groaned. Another group! Was there going to be a summer of warring groups? The man told Ken to stop following him and so Ken went back to his place.

Ken stewed about this latest fiasco in the making. He didn't want to go into Wonder and witness what might be happening there. He didn't have long to wait for information. Ellie phoned him to tell him that the End of Times group had decided to camp in Wonder's only park. The whole group was being very disruptive and the leader, who called himself Prophet Joel, had blasted away on his bullhorn at the gathered crowd of townspeople. The crowd had become angry and had circled the prophet and his people and the situation was getting dangerous. The police had been called. Ellie had to go but told Ken to hurry into town.

When Ken arrived there was no group to be seen. The park was empty and only a few townspeople were on the streets talking in small groups. He asked a man who was standing alone where the prophet's group had gone. He shrugged his shoulders and muttered that the police had shooed them out of town. Ken wondered where they had gone to and where they might be hiding. He felt sure that the prophet wouldn't have gone very far. He went back home and kept thinking about the Prophet Joel. As he was preparing a light supper he thought he heard something. He looked out his back door. There seemed to be some movement in the trees that bordered the back of his property. He saw flashes of different colors and then he saw orange! Oh, now he knew where this loony group had decided to camp! He decided to spy on them for a while. Sure enough, he could make out the outlines of tents. That property was owned by a member of the Town Council of Wonder! It was going to be developed in the near future. Quickly he grabbed his phone to call John Townshead, the owner of the property. John was at home and he said that he would come right away with the police.

It was getting dark by the time the "posse" arrived. They all gathered in Ken's kitchen to discuss their plan of action. It was agreed that the best plan was for them to come upon the group suddenly. They all ducked down and gradually made their way to the edge of the encampment. They looked through the bushes to see the prophet holding forth to about fifteen people. A huge fire was roaring and they all sat around it while the prophet stood to the side of it. The way the fire and shadows played over his features and form created a fantastic sight. He mesmerized the onlookers both by the fire and those hiding in the bushes. The officer in charge jabbed John to tell him that they'd better get into action. Then the officer gave the agreed upon signal and the entire posse jumped into the firelight. The prophet stopped in mid sentence with his hand pointed to the sky and his people jumped to their feet and ran in all directions. What happened next was hard to believe. As quick as a flash the prophet grabbed a burning log and threw it at his attackers. That log started a fire in the brush and before long the edge of the forest was burning with great intensity. Then the prophet disappeared. In the end the entire group got away. The would-be posse had to call the Wonder Fire Department to put out the fire. The posse was angry at the escape of yet another troublemaking group of nutters. Everyone felt that they had not seen the last of them.

A few weeks later the students returned and the sound of hammers and drills and saws was heard to all hours. Ken hated the disturbance that all this noise had brought to his quiet life. He had gone to the Mayor several times to complain about letting the group develop the property for questionable reasons. He merely replied that until criminal actions or threats to the community occurred, he could not bring any actions against them. The land had been legally purchased. They were not squatters as long as the owner let them stay there. Ken heard them working late into the night. It seemed that they worked all night. There were backhoes and trucks and all kinds of equipment on the property. Ken was puzzled as to exactly what they were building. He could not see anything because they had erected a fifteen foot wall all around the property. Why the mystery?

June came and Ken was working in his vegetable garden one day when he heard a familiar sound. It was not a sound he wanted to hear at all. He raced to the front of his house and there he witnessed the Prophet Joel leading his little flock back and forth along the front wall that faced the road in front of the construction site. He was shouting out about the fire of God and punishment. The scary thing about this was that each person was carrying a flaming torch! Before Ken could get help the group started to try to set the wooden wall on fire and some threw their torches over the wall. Soon there were shouts from inside the wall and a huge fire was roaring both on the wall and inside it in the construction area. The flock and their Prophet high-tailed it down the road heading away from Wonder. The gate to the compound opened with students running screaming out of it after the departing arsonists who were able to elude their pursuers. The fire was dowsed by those on the inside and the blackened, fatigued students limped back inside their mysterious construction site. Ken had witnessed the whole episode. He was thinking about the fact that this crazy group must be very athletic to be able to leave any situation so quickly.

Ken had no communication with his neighbors. They came to and from their construction site and never ventured near his place. Ken didn't really want to talk to them but he was always on pins and needles as to what may occur next. The fire incident had come all too close to being a real emergency. What if the Prophet returned at night? Maybe the whole forest would be set on fire and even burn down his house? He phoned the Mayor about this real possibility. He said that he'd send patrol cars to patrol the area for the next few months. Ken felt a little better about the situation but only a little bit. The construction sounds next door had died down and this made Ken wonder even more about what they were up to inside those tall walls.

Chapter Fifteen
The Silence Broken

Ken grew increasingly suspicious about the lack of noise from his usually busy neighbors. He did not hear any sound at all. Where were they? The Prophet and his flock had not been seen since the wall fire episode. The quiet was creepy. No Prophet, no noise and no one around. No one seemed to be at the compound anymore. It was late June and all Ken heard was the chirping of birds and the occasional cry of eagles way up high playing diving games. Once in a while a vehicle would drive up and enter the compound but no one seemed to venture out on their own. Vehicles came and went but only sporadically and Ken surmised that it was either to get or to deliver supplies. Perhaps they were working away from the site. He couldn't imagine where they would be working. His curiosity finally got the better of him and he decided he'd investigate. He planned a night "raid".

At dusk he set out to advance towards the fence and to try to peer through it. He finally was able to find a small hole. He was able to see the structure that looked complete. He wasn't sure what it was because it was all angles. Maybe it wasn't a sphinx. He listened very carefully and he thought that he heard some muffled sounds coming from across the compound. He thought he detected a machine working far away but it seemed under the ground. Yes, it was coming from a place underground! They were digging underground! Why? He sat in thought for a while and then it came to him what they were trying to accomplish. They were digging a tunnel to the mountain! What an undertaking! They had about three miles to cover. Ken sat in the darkness trying to digest this latest revelation. What would motivate them to dig a tunnel to the mountain?

After Ken got back to his house he sat in his favorite chair with his cats and he thought and thought. Should he reveal this information or not? He went to bed undecided. The next day he still didn't know what to do. He wanted them to be caught on the mountain. Technically they weren't on the mountain. They were digging under other people's property. That was illegal. He was perplexed about this situation. He wanted to see what they would achieve and therefore part of him wanted to keep this a secret. The next day a new load of students appeared and then disappeared into the compound. Ken wondered if Star was in that group. What would the students do if they were confronted? Ken was restless all that day and the next. Finally he went to talk to someone he trusted to keep his secret.

The next day Ken knocked on Ellie's door and she cheerfully ushered him into her comfortable living room. She had just finished working at Sweet Treats. It was a continuing to be a huge success. She gabbed about all the latest news in the apartments and about the best selling doughnuts. Finally she stopped talking and asked Ken what he had on his mind. When he told her about his suspicions she was aghast with surprise. After talking about the activities of the group, they both came to the conclusion that perhaps the situation should be monitored for a while before revealing their secret. Ken was still uneasy about it all but he left Ellie's place knowing that she wouldn't tell a soul.

About a week later there seemed to be activity in the compound. A big bonfire was burning and it appeared that a celebration was taking place. Drums were beaten and laughter and loud talking assailed Ken's ears. After the GREAT SILENCE this was an unwelcome change. The celebration went on all night and Ken got not one wink of sleep. The next day all was silence again. Ken crept over to his hole in the wall (which he had "made") that night and observed a few lights in the structure but nothing else. Everyone seemed to have deserted the place again. He wondered if they knew what to do to actually dig a safe tunnel. How would they reinforce it? When they got nearer to the mountain they would probably need dynamite. He agonized over whether he should tell the authorities about these activities. He knew in his heart that he'd have to tell the truth. What if some of the students got hurt? He'd feel responsible.

Several days later a cement truck rolled up to the compound. Ken surmised that they were going to use cement to stabilize the tunnel. Who owned the cement truck? Did the driver of the cement truck know what was going on or would he just deliver the cement and leave? About an hour later the truck left. Maybe the driver didn't have a clue about the activities. Ken had to know more and so he set up a little campsite of sorts just outside the fence where he was hidden by some low bushes. He definitely heard digging noises and heavy machinery going full blast day and night. He sometimes saw the students in the building eating meals or taking naps. They all seemed on a tight schedule and there was no fooling around. It was all business. Ken now knew enough and he would have to report what he knew as soon as possible.

The next day Ken met with the Mayor and told him everything. The Mayor was dismayed to say the least and called the local police chief. A search warrant was obtained and a posse set out for the "mine". It was getting dark when everyone arrived as quietly as possible. A bullhorn was used to attract the attention of those inside the compound. There was no response. After about thirty minutes the gate was forced open and the posse entered the enclosed area. The immense structure was dark and silent. Everyone fanned out and the entrance to the work area was found and cautiously they entered a tunnel which descended into the ground and away into darkness. They inched their way down the dimly lit tunnel and gradually they began to hear sounds of machinery at work. Carefully they moved forward and then suddenly they saw the students working away at the walls of the tunnel just ahead. They were so busy shoveling and packing mud and a cement mixture that they were not aware of the onlookers. A small cement mixer was grinding away and they could not have heard the approaching posse. Finally, the workers were forced to look up when the posse was quite literally in their faces. The students dropped what they were doing and began to run but this time they were all stopped.

The whole crew was hauled into town and thrown into jail cells. They had been illegally digging a tunnel and that was enough to have them detained. There were loud shouts about getting their city lawyers into Wonder and showing how wrongfully they had been treated. Their cries of indignation were ignored. The professor was nowhere to be found. Did he get away? He was probably in Monza. Ken was glad that he had told the truth about what had been going on but he wasn't sure if all would be settled peacefully. By now all of Wonder had heard about the tunnel and crowds were milling outside the police station. Some had placards about getting kooks out of Wonder for good. The Mayor was nervous and ordered the crowds dispersed. When Monza T.V. reporters came to Wonder the Mayor refused to give interviews and told them to go away. This did not stop them from trying to interview anyone who would talk. Some people did talk and a twisted story emerged about Wonder. More reporters came to Wonder and the story got even wilder. The silence had been broken but now there was a thunderstorm of confusion and chaos.

Chapter Sixteen
Cave Dwellers

It was the day after the big capture of students that all kinds of events happened. First of all, the students had found a way of escape! It seemed impossible for all of them to disappear but they did and their cells were found empty. Somehow they were able to pry open the windows of their cells. They probably had some sort of small tools that had not been found on them or they weren't really searched. They must have got away about two in the morning. Their guards had fallen asleep. The cells were found empty about six in the morning. A lot of blame was thrown around but the fact was that the prisoners had vanished. A large mob of officials, policemen and citizens fanned out to search for them. Ken was part of one group searching around his home area. Nothing had changed at the compound. The police had taped off the entire area. The tunnel had been searched to its furthest point and then it was sealed. The students couldn't have gone there and so everyone was madly looking in all directions. Of course the press was following all of this frenzied activity with the greatest of interest and annoying everyone trying to find the escapees. The biggest liars in the town were having the time of their lives making up fantastic stories for the wide-eyed reporters. These stories brought even more reporters and those who were curious. Wonder's two hotels were stuffed full of "outsiders". The town was experiencing an economic boom of sorts with all the increased spending by the "visitors" and "tourists".

Ken was so weary of it all. Just when Wonder had sort of settled down, yet another stupid series of events had occurred. Now Wonder was becoming infamous. Someone had put up a huge sign just out of town proclaiming that Wonder was the Cult Capital of the World. Other signs proclaimed guided tours of tantalizing sites where cults had lived. Ken knew who these "sign-producers" were and he knew where they lived. Some of them had been involved in some of the old groups that had left long ago. They had found a way to make money. They were going to milk this craze for all its worth. Ken thought he had seen it all when he witnessed a group of twenty people being led by a Wonder citizen to look at the strange sphinx-like building of the "Egyptian" group. It was getting to be a circus!

A week passed and the escapees had not been found. Search parties were looking everywhere imaginable. It seemed as if they had vanished off the face of the Earth. Ken had not involved himself in any of the searches. He was totally finished with what he called "nonsense". He went on with his quiet life but it was often interrupted with news reporters and curious groups led to the site of the Great Tunnel. There was even a summer fair going on in town with an Egyptian theme. There were rides and games and treats all centered on ancient Egypt. It drew great crowds. Wonder had never had so many outsiders. Businesses were booming.

The search parties were called off after a few more days. Ken breathed a sigh of relief. Maybe things would get back to normal and the visitors would leave the area. By mid August it seemed that the craziness had gone from the town and the area surrounding it. There were no more tourists and no "side shows". The Mayor had to put his foot down and he had declared an end to the madness. The summer ended on a peaceful note and everyone tried to get on with their lives and to look forward to the future.

Meanwhile, the students were living in caves and watching the town from their vantage point. They had not dropped their quest. They looked down on Wonder and smiled. They were where they wanted to be and they were building their "kingdom" in another place. All was going well. The cave dwellers got supplies by theft and stealth. Soon businesses and homeowners in Wonder were reporting break-ins. Food was the main item stolen the most often. Then people noticed that bedding and utensils and tools went missing. A Community Watch was set up to try and catch the thieves. Somehow the thieves were too quick and they always got away. Putting two and two together caused the town to realize that the students were the culprits. Ken heard about this latest news and he inwardly felt sick. He was very, very tired. He wanted to get away.

One night he heard a commotion near his house and he got up quickly and looked out of his back window and to his surprise he saw lights around the sealed-off compound. The students were back! It sounded like they were tearing down something very fast. Ken phoned the local police and waited for them to arrive. It took them ten minutes to come and there were only two patrol cars. Lights were flashing and loud voices blared and guns were drawn. Ken watched it all unfold. Orie was barking and the cats were howling. The students came out of the compound with their hands in the air. However, several had got away into the darkness. Ken thought to himself that it was all happening again. Some were caught and some escaped. It was the same scenario being played over again.

The prisoners were taken to the Wonder jail and this time extra guards were put on duty around the clock. There was no escape this time. They were finally carted off to Monza to stand trial and they all had to serve time in the Big House but it was only for a few months. The other escapees had not been found. They were busy bees. They were cave dwellers and they had a plan.

While everyone was interested in the trial and the imprisonment of the captured students, the escapees had been making crude tunnels that connected several caves deep inside White Mountain. They still stole and scrounged around for food and supplies and they had everything they needed to survive the winter. They had built their "kingdom" and their dwelling places were found inside the vast mountain. There were seven of them and one was Star. They were wild and unapproachable.

Chapter Seventeen
Winter Mischief

Ken was planning a special Christmas. He wanted all of his friends over for a wonderful, traditional feast. He was baking many delights. As the snow fell outside his window he felt so content. Everything was so peaceful and quiet. The snow was getting higher. Orie loved to jump through the drifts and then come into the house and shake snow and water all over the kitchen. The cats gingerly stepped into the snow and then ran back into the house. Ken laughed when he saw them stare at the snow with big eyes. No news was heard about any unusual events in the area and so all surmised that their last "war" was over. Surely the students had scurried back to Monza and were enjoying the warmth of their dorms. No one thought that any of them could possibly be around the Wonder area.

A week before Christmas Ken went into town to buy a few simple gifts. He met Ellie in the drugstore. She was looking forward to the party. She was full of life and happy. They were talking by the front store window when Ken suddenly saw someone looking into it. The person was scruffy and dirty and looked wild. He couldn't tell if it was a man or woman. The eyes were piercing like those of an animal. Ken shuddered. He motioned Ellie to look at the stranger. She gasped and stared and then went toward the window. The "creature" looked scared and then ran away quickly down the street. Ellie and Ken had never seen such a strange sight. They ran onto the street but the stranger had vanished. They both looked at each other and didn't know what to make of just what had happened. They were shaking from the encounter. Ken thought that this creature could be one of the students but then he put it out of his mind. It couldn't have been a student. He was so wrong.

Ken kept a lookout for any more strange-looking creatures and saw none until Christmas eve. He had eaten his supper and he was now baking some Christmas cookies. Suddenly, he happened to see something out of the corner of his eye. There was something taking place outside his kitchen window. He hurried to the window and peered out into the darkness. He saw two figures going around the corner of the house. Quickly Ken raced to the front corner window and he saw that the figures were staring right back at him! Ken was transfixed by the wild stares of weird creatures and that was what they looked like as he stood there almost paralyzed with fear. Then one of these strange beings started to pound on the window! Ken quickly pulled his curtains shut. Then he shut all of the curtains on all of the living room windows. The windows were all pounded on and Ken was afraid that they'd break them soon. Orie was barking madly and trying to get out of the front door. She was scratching at it and jumping on it. The cats had long ago scurried under Ken's bed. Ken heard shouts and heard snowballs being thrown at his house. All this racket was kept up for about half an hour and then everything was very quiet. Ken carefully pulled back a corner of a curtain on the front window. He had turned on the porch light and as he looked out of the window he could make out footprints in the snow. These footprints were made by boots. These creatures were humans. Ken confirmed to himself that these people were most likely, the students trying to get supplies. He hadn't figured out where they were living but he did know that they were desperately hungry and in need of warmth. He felt bad that he hadn't invited them in but he wasn't sure about their mental states.

Yet another search was carried out to find where these creatures were holed up but it was to no avail and the search was called off and Christmas was celebrated in the homes in the community. Ken's party went off with great success. He beat everyone at Monopoly. He was crowned King of Monopoly and a rematch was scheduled to see if he could be unseated from his "throne". Even though he had had great fun with his friends, Ken couldn't get the creatures out of his mind. He knew that they were in utter need and here he was feasting and having great fun while they shivered and starved in some God-forsaken place.

In a dark, dank and frosty cave sat seven souls. They didn't move and they didn't speak. All of their food had run out and only a small fire burned in front of them. They drank snow water and that was all they had and they had run out of energy to forage for food. Only one person had volunteered to go on a food hunt and he was trying to get up the strength to set forth that very night. It was a few days after Christmas and it was now or never if they were going to be able to live another day. Ralph was the chosen food-finder and slowly he got up and stumbled towards the entrance to the cave. He was going to get food that night. Nothing was going to stop him from coming back with loads of provisions. He had a sledge which he dragged by a rope. The others waved at him feebly as he set out into the darkness under a full moon. His beard had grown down to his chest and it was covered with frost. His clothes were tattered and torn and not warm enough for the severe weather he faced. As quickly as he able to manage, which involved many falls and slow recoveries, he headed down the mountain and towards Ken's home. This time force would be applied. His clan was dying.

As he neared Ken's place he noticed that all was dark. It would be good if no one was at home. After forcing open the front door Ralph headed towards the kitchen. Suddenly Orie jumped on him and knocked him to the floor. As Ralph got up he noticed a small table nearby and he grabbed it and hit Orie so hard with it that the poor dog was soon unconscious. Ralph quickly set to work and raided the refrigerator and cupboards. Luckily there were a lot of leftovers from the Christmas feast and soon Ralph had loaded his sledge high with enough food to last them for quite a while. Ken was one who liked to stock up and so Ralph reaped the benefits of this habit. Ralph threw a tarp over the high mound of provisions and fastened it securely and off he went into the frosty night. Orie came to and moaned. Ralph was halfway to the cave when Ken came home from his visit in town.

Ken soon found Orie and realized what had happened. Nearly everything seemed to be destroyed or stolen. Ken knew it was the work of the students. What was to be done? Was the town in for a winter of mischief? Ken had to talk to the Mayor again. He took Orie to the vet the next day and he assured Ken that his beloved dog was going to be fine. After leaving Orie at home, he went to talk to the Mayor. The Mayor was going to put out more patrols for the next while. He felt that sooner or later that the students would be caught because they obviously needed supplies. Ken was upset that he had to buy a lot of food. He had not banked on having to do a lot more baking and food preparation. He liked to prepare all his own meals and so he had a lot of work ahead of him. Orie was supposed to keep a low profile for awhile as she had a mild concussion.

For the next week Ken was busy baking and cooking. It had snowed a lot and the snowdrifts were high. He was almost cut off from civilization. A plow had turned up in the middle of the week and Ken was able to shovel out to the road. It had also turned bitterly cold. Ken wondered about the 'creature thieves' and how they were getting along, wherever they were hiding. Surely they had left the area in a state of great desperation. Little did he know that the cave dwellers had decided to winter in a warmer area until the spring. Their location was very near Ken.

Chapter Eighteen
Abducted

The students came to a bitter decision. They would die in the cave unless they left it and found a warmer shelter. They decided that they would come back to their original building and forage for food and supplies from it. They all agreed that no one would know that they had returned to the building. Under the cover of darkness they entered into their old abode. They were happy to enter it even though it was bare and cheerless. Anything would be better than the cave. They lit a fire in the crude fireplace and warmed their fingers and toes. They needed food and they knew of a wonderful food source. In fact, they had decided that Ken's house would be their house and that Ken would be captured by them to be their cook and that all his possessions would be theirs to enjoy.

The next morning they all burst into Ken's house and captured him quickly before he could think straight. They took over and he was kept tied up. Now Ken was really afraid about what would happen. They seemed particularly frenzied, not to mention the terrible odor that emitted from them as they tore about his home grabbing food and talking loudly. They ordered him to cook them a sumptuous feast as they were "Egyptian royalty" (their words) and deserved such a treat.

Ken was glad to get untied and to keep busy but all the while his mind was trying to figure out a way of escape. Ken had noticed a scruffy-looking female who looked vaguely familiar even though her face was encrusted with dirt and her hair was knotted and greasy. Could it be Star? He peered furtively at her as he chopped carrots. He convinced himself that indeed it was her and that she didn't want anything to do with him. She was laughing at one of the young men and teasing him about how much he was going to devour. They all started yelling at Ken to get the feast cooked. Ken quickly put together a very sumptuous feast and soon it was on the table and it was attacked by the pack. They acted like starved wolves. All civilized behaviour had been abandoned long ago. Ken was nauseated by them. He wanted to get away, fast. He told them that he was going to put some scraps in the garbage outside. They didn't seem too pay much attention to him as he grabbed his coat and set out for the back yard. He, however had other plans.

Quickly he ran to his truck and jumped in it and headed for town as fast as he could travel. The students hadn't seemed to have noticed him and so he had been able to get away without any delay. He went straight to the Police Station and several squad cars followed him back to his house. When they arrived back at his house Ken was surprised to find it empty. It had been trashed but no one was to be found. They all headed toward the old encampment but nothing was stirring there either. It was all too strange. Where could they have gone? Surely they wouldn't have gone back to the cave that they had described as cold and miserable. After a thorough search of the area, Ken was left to clean up the huge mess in his house. They had demolished every piece of furniture and took every scrap of food. His place was uninhabitable. He took his cats and dog with him and headed for town. Ellie offered to put him up until he had figured out what to do about his house.

Ken decided that he wouldn't live in his house that winter. Over the next few days he boarded it up and he hoped that it wouldn't be touched. He'd go back in the spring and completely renovate it. He planned to check on it periodically. He was so frustrated over not being able to live in his own home. Ellie was able to give him one of her bedrooms and she enjoyed the pets. Ken was despondent. These crazy people always seemed to interfere with his life. He never wanted to see them again. Star had gone completely mad, he thought. She was very mixed up and Ken wondered what would happen to her in the wilderness.

Several weeks later Ken went to check on his house. He found fresh footprints in the snow around the front of it. He hoped against hope that no one was there inside. He opened the back door and peered inside at the darkness. He saw a dark form coming towards him. It was Star! She told him to wait and that she would explain. Ken motioned her to come outside. Star came slowly, like an old crippled woman. Ken could tell that she was in a serious condition. Star weakly muttered that she wanted to go to her mother's place. Ken carried her to his truck and laid her on the back seat. He headed straight toward the hospital. They admitted her quickly and treatment was started. Ken rushed to her mother's house and brought her to the hospital. Star's mother, Lily, cried when she saw the state that her daughter was in and from that day until she was fully recovered, she rarely left her side.

Ken was sorry for Star but that was all he felt. She and her "gang" had caused such a lot of trouble in the community. He hoped that she would recover and get the help she needed but he didn't want anything more to do with her ever again. Star did recover but she had to be sent to a hospital in the city for her complete recovery. It was a psychiatric hospital. Star was not herself and it was possible that she would never again be the sunny girl that she once was when she lived in Wonder. Ken felt that it was a time so long ago. Her mother was so upset and forlorn that people were worried about her mental state. Sad and almost disengaged from reality, one day she left Wonder. Everyone who knew her was surprised and dismayed. A cloud of unhappiness settled over the community.

Chapter Nineteen
More Strangers and a Move

As the winter days came and went Ken wondered about many things. What was he doing in this town? He was free to go anywhere but he felt restless and rooted at the same time. He needed a big change in his life. He was now thirty years old and he wanted to accomplish something but he didn't know what it was and where he would do it. His artwork had sold well and so he settled on producing paintings. Ellie's apartment was overflowing with them. Painting pictures kept Ken busy but he still was uneasy about several things. He had painted many mountain pictures. He was always drawn to them in a strange way, almost beyond his control.

One sunny day in early March, Ken was sitting in an open area painting White Mountain. As he sketched away his eye caught something on the horizon near the trees at the base of the mountain. It looked like tents. He grabbed his binoculars and looked again and sure enough there were several tents clustered together. Ken felt his heart fall. It couldn't be **THEM**! Would they never leave? As he intensified the magnification on his binoculars he noticed that several people were milling around in front of one of the tents. As he crept closer he could make out several familiar figures. It was the students! A big fire was roaring and it looked like they were warming themselves by it and drinking coffee and having a wonderful time together. Why would they want to come back again and live near the mountain? Why were they intent on living in primitive conditions?

Ken was so disgusted with them that he packed up and left for town. He had to get away from this place! He planned on leaving for good. He was thoroughly fed up with the constant struggle with strange people doing strange and dangerous things. He wanted to go somewhere safe and untouched by weirdos. He thought about the possibilities before him and as he tossed on his bed he came to the decision to leave for a little town to the north of Wonder. He was sure no one would want to come there to set up a colony for their cause. He finally fell asleep knowing what he had to do to move on with his life.

The next morning Ken informed Ellie about what he intended to do and she was shocked and dismayed. She told him that he wouldn't escape weird people as they were found everywhere. His home had been rented out to a local handyman and he had lived there from shortly after the time Star had been found in the house. He had been fixing it up. Ken would decide what to do with it when it was completed. He told her that he felt that a new start elsewhere was what he needed and so he started to pack. He packed up all that day and filled his truck up to capacity. He would come back for his cats and dog when he was settled. Ellie was sobbing into her handkerchief and several of his Open Arms friends came to see him off. There were many tears and sad faces. Ken was gulping and fighting back tears as he drove away from the town he had lived in for so many years. Perhaps he'd be back. He only knew that he needed a break from the madness of this place. A new perspective and a new adventure was what he needed.

He drove north to a town called Deep Valley. This looked like a town in which he could settle down for a while. As he drove into the town he was happy to see normal looking people. He didn't see anyone in strange colors and there were no groups clumped together whispering and planning. He went to the real estate office and was able by the end of the day, to call a small house just out of the town, his very own. It had two acres, lots of trees and the nearest neighbor was two miles away. This would be perfect. He moved in after two weeks of waiting for the paperwork to be finalized. He stayed at the local motel and he was very glad to leave it and its restaurant "meals". He was able to unload his possessions quite quickly. The house had been uninhabited for a while and so he aired it out and set to work to clean it. The next day he bought some furniture and groceries and he was very satisfied with himself at how quickly he had been able to set up his new home. He set out for Wonder to get his cats and his dog.

His friends were very glad to see him and were surprised at how quickly he had set up his new residence. They all wanted to visit him as soon as possible. Ken gave them all an open invitation to come whenever they were in the area. There was some local news, too. Apparently, the tent dwellers had moved closer to town and were raiding the town. Same old story. Ken was weary beyond words. He didn't want to know anymore about them and their "doings". He said his farewells and headed north. His animals were safely in his truck and all was well. He hummed a happy tune and patted his dog sitting next to him. Suddenly he veered his truck out of the path of an oncoming van. It had been heading straight for him! It headed into a ditch and Ken stopped to see if everyone was all right. As he neared the van he noticed that they all were dressed in yellow. No one seemed hurt and some of them were laughing and giggling. Ken remembered that sound and then he put two and two together and thought that he knew these people. Ken felt the same familiar feeling of dread mixed with disgust. Were these people from the Yellow Group? Did they live in Deep Valley? Ken told them that he would call a tow truck when he got into town. They thanked him and they kept joking about their predicament.

Ken called the local tow truck and it set out to rescue the Yellow Group. Ken had recognized some familiar faces. The Yellow Group had left Wonder several months ago and he wondered where they had relocated. He didn't have long to wait to find out the answer to that question. He was in the local hardware store the next day when he spotted two of them. They rushed over to him and thanked him profusely for assisting them in their time of need. Ken asked where they lived and he was informed that the whole group lived together at the eastern edge of the town. They invited him to visit them. Ken mumbled something about being busy and made a quick retreat. He was wondering to himself if he had moved to the wrong town. He didn't have long to wait to find out what kind of town Deep Valley was and who lived in it.

It was two weeks later when Ken found out some other facts about this area he now lived in and what he learned troubled him. Apparently the nearest neighbors were members of another group. He went to call on them to introduce himself and he found out that they were the Red Group! The Red Group had been ousted as they had lost the duel and this is where they had landed! What if other Groups from Wonder had settled in Deep Valley, too? Ken sat staring out of his kitchen window and wondered if he could escape any of their "activities". Surely they wouldn't be up to their old tricks, or would they? He tried to remember what the Red Group believed in and then he remembered that they were the hummers. He also remembered that Brother Joyous was the name of the Yellow Group's leader. These groups didn't seem to remember Ken and maybe that was because he had grown a beard and gained a little weight. Ken sat staring outside for a long while until the sun set behind the valley.

Chapter Twenty
The Valley of Escape

Ken soon learned that the valley had significance for the groups. It was their place of refuge! The town was very tolerant towards all kinds of people and everyone seemed to get along quite well. The main industry was logging and tourists passed through the town and were given tours of old mining towns nearby and other places of interest. As in Wonder there was a special place and that was the top of the valley. It was called the Valley Ridge by the locals. If one would trek up there and get to the top of the valley a spectacular view awaited. At night bonfires could often be seen on the Ridge. Ken didn't want to go up there as he knew he'd surely meet kooks.

Ken had met some "normal" people and he was determined to make friends with "safe" people and to stay out of local politics and concerns. All he wanted was peace and quiet. He had started to paint again and he was planning to go to Monza in a few weeks for an art show. He had invited a nice couple over for dinner and he was planning a great meal for the occasion. Yes, he'd keep out of any "funny business" the groups might be up to and they'd not be a part of his new life.

Ruth and John Moss came over one Saturday night and they had a great time all together. They were teachers at the local school and they had lived in Deep Valley for five years. Ken had struck up a conversation in the local grocery store and they had hit it off and soon were in contact on a regular basis. They warned Ken about the strange groups in the area and Ken assured them that he knew more than he wanted to know about them. They warned Ken that there was a division in the town. The insiders were those who lived there to raise their families and live a quiet small town life and then there were the outsiders who had suddenly arrived several years ago. Ken didn't inform them about what he had experienced in Wonder. He wanted a fresh start. The less time spent discussing the groups, the better! Ruth and John warned Ken that the groups had caused a lot of trouble. Ken could have guessed that that was the case! He changed the subject and shortly afterwards said goodbye and promised to drop in to see them when he was in town the next time.

Several of Ken's friends from Wonder came to visit him the next weekend and they stayed overnight. They all approved of his new digs. Ken did not mention the Groups. Ken felt lonely after they left and he half wondered if he had made the right move. He'd give this place a try before he came to a verdict. Ellie's words about weirdos everywhere rang through his mind like a blast of cold air. He only knew that he planned to stay far away from them. How could he have forgotten that in small communities it is hard to escape from people? He found out that truth when he met some Yellow Group members in the Post Office. They approached him and they began to chat on and on about some up coming event. Ken didn't want to listen and so he made excuses and wanly smiled as he tried to create as much distance from them as he could within the confines of the small building. He dashed out the door only to be met by another "Yellow" who cheerfully smiled and waved and giggled as he trudged through the snow. Ken felt a headache coming on and he drove his truck out of town as quickly as possible.

Ken soon learned that the Brown Group was living on the far west side of the town in their own compound. They had their own greenhouses and the sold plants and garden necessities. They called it the Good Earth Nursery. Even though Ken would need gardening supplies and plants he didn't plan to purchase them at that particular place! Ken felt more depressed as he realized that the kooks from Wonder had settled right where he now lived! What as he going to do? Fortunately he lived far away from them and so he felt safe for the moment.

Ken went to Monza for his art show. He was a hit and all of his paintings sold. Ken was more than self-sufficient from the art show money and the steady rents that came from the apartments in Wonder. He also was collecting rent from his house just outside of Wonder. The art gallery wanted him to put on a show in another city nearby called Fernwood. This show would be in August. As he was discussing the plans for this show a young lady entered the front door of the gallery. She looked vaguely familiar. She slowly moved around the room looking carefully at his paintings. She stood a long time in front of a large painting of Black Mountain. As Ken observed her out of the corner of his eye, she turned around and he saw her face clearly. It was Star! She looked fine. He didn't know what to say and so he hurriedly excused himself and left out of the back door of the gallery. Why was she allowed out of the hospital? Could she be better or had she left without permission? He couldn't get her out of his mind as he drove to his hotel.

Ken left the next day for his home. He kept brushing away any thoughts of Star. He wanted to find a new special friend and someday he would marry and have children. Star would not be his wife. There was too much negative history between them and besides she was mentally unbalanced. Ken told himself these things as the snow softly fell on his truck's window and the sky went darker and darker and the snow fell deeper and deeper. It was one of those early spring freak snowstorms. He was about ten miles from town when his truck stalled and then stopped. Snow was piling up and it was getting colder. Ken had prepared for any such emergency but he didn't relish the thought of spending the night in his truck. He was able to call the tow truck company in Deep Valley but they said that they couldn't come until the morning. Ken was able to get only a few hours of sleep and in the morning he sat patiently waiting for the tow truck to appear. The road had not been plowed and the snowdrifts were up to his truck door windows. He called the tow truck company but they told him that they couldn't come until the road was cleared. Ken was getting worried. He decided to walk to his place. He gathered what he could carry in a knapsack he had in his truck. After fighting with the snow he was able to dig his way out of the truck. The snow on the road was up to his knees!

As he plunged through the snow he realized that it was going to be hard work to get to his place. It was now about nine o'clock and not one plow was to be seen. No one was traveling today. After another hour of falling and slipping and struggling, Ken was exhausted. He was able to see some buildings up ahead and he realized that it was the Red Group's farm. Ken resolved that he'd try to get there and get some help. Finally, after what seemed to take forever, Ken stumbled into the cleared driveway of his neighbours. He knocked on their front door.

The leader of the group opened the door and smiled at Ken and then looked concerned. Quickly Ken was ushered into a large kitchen with a huge fireplace that was roaring hot. Various busy females waited on him and helped him out of his sopping wet outer garments and one of them pushed a steaming mug of hot chocolate in front of him. Ken soon warmed up and explained his situation. They told him that the town plow had broken down but that they had their own plow and would help him to his place and plow it out and then try to get his truck back to his place. They told him not to worry and that they had the resources necessary to get his truck back to him safely. Ken was astonished at their generosity and was humbled by their kindness.

True to their words, the Reds had his truck back to him by that evening and Ken had his driveway plowed and they had even bought him some groceries. Ken was deeply grateful. There was no way that he could ignore these people completely after all of their many acts of charity on his behalf. He promised to drop in for a visit with them, soon.

Chapter Twenty-One
Past Deeds

After the snowstorm it seemed that winter had had enough and it was now time for Spring to appear. The snow melted and never returned. As was the predictable cycle, grass started to get green and grow and buds appeared on trees and plants. Birds happily chirped. The sun beamed down in brilliant splendor. Ken loved this time of year. He had a long list of plans for his property. He was going to purchase some goats and chickens and geese but he had to make sure he had proper buildings to house these animals. He hired one of the Reds to build him a barn and chicken and geese pens. His name was Joseph Rodin and he was the same age as Ken. Ken and Joseph had long talks about many things as they worked side by side day after day. He told Ken that the group was trying to forget the events in Wonder and to get on with achieving happiness. He said that some of the older members would bring up things from the past and they would be hushed by the others. However, the group's goal was to ascend Valley Ridge without trying! That's when Ken almost lost it. Even though it sounded that clearer minds now prevailed in the group, the idea of finding "something" in a high place was ever before them and motivated them to achieve it. Ken asked Joseph how they would ascend the valley without trying at all. Joseph just smiled and said that they would all know when the time was right to hum themselves up it and then true bliss would be achieved!

Ken really liked Joseph and so he never brought up the "ascension" again. The buildings were all built and now it was time for the livestock purchases. He had to go into town to buy his chickens and geese from some of the Green group. Yes, they too, were living in the outskirts of this town. They raised animals and sold some of them. Ken searched his memory for what he knew about these people. They had been involved in many failed attempts up Black Mountain and then there was the business about the illegal mine and their involvement with the Brown Group in illegal activities. They were really running away from their unlawful, crime - laden pasts! Ken wondered what he should do and then realized that it would all be too much for local authorities to believe if he told them. As he neared their compound he was filled with conflicting thoughts about having to deal with them and he wondered if they would remember him.

As he drove down the long dirt road towards a rambling house he saw that there were children playing in the field next to it and he wondered why they weren't in school. He knocked on the front door and waited. He waited and waited. Finally, just as he was going to turn away the door opened and a smiling woman greeted him. Ken didn't recognize her and so he plunged into his reasons for being there and she ushered him into the living room area to wait for her husband. She offered him some coffee and a doughnut. As Ken munched his doughnut he looked around the room and slowly came to the realization that many people lived in this home. Pictures of family groups and many pieces of furniture were scattered around the room. He saw several other women going to and from the kitchen area. A happy buzz of chatter could be heard amid the clatter of pots and pans. It was getting towards lunch time and lunch was being prepared.

Finally, Ben, the lady's husband, came and introduced himself to Ken. As it was nearing the lunch hour he invited Ken to eat with them. After lunch they would select the geese and chickens. Ken agreed and sat talking to Ben at the kitchen table. Around noon the children poured in and sat politely at their places. Several other men came and finally everyone was seated. Ben addressed the "air" in a speech about the wide open country spaces and the bountiful Earth and then everyone dug into the delicious repast. The vegetable soup was superb and the buns were immense and filled with nuts and currants. Ben boasted that they grew all they needed and they had little need to go to town for provisions. The salad was crisp and filled with several homegrown vegetables. They had a huge greenhouse and stored vegetables in a cellar or froze them and put them into a freezer along with some frozen fruit. Ken inquired as to why the children were at home and Ben told him that they were home schooled and taught by two of the women who were former teachers. He told Ken that he thought the children needed to taught the 'proper respect for the planet' and this was the place for them. There were four families living together in apparent harmony. All of them looked cheerful and contented. Ken thought to himself that they looked too contented. Was it a show for him? He didn't recognize any of them as the people who had lived in Wonder. This must be a "new generation" or an offshoot of the original group.

Ken was able to get several geese and a dozen chickens that day for a good price. He noted that the compound looked well-run and carefully maintained. He was invited back any time he wanted to stop by and he was promised another great meal. This place seemed to be a utopia of sorts. Was it all too good to be true? He wondered if they believed the same things as the 'original' group. Had they morphed into a new ideology? Had their ideology changed to suit new circumstances? Where was the 'old guard'? Ken had many questions.

Ken's next mission was to find two goats. He did some research on goats and found out that goats were being sold at a local goat farm. It produced cheese and milk for sale and goats were also sold at reasonable prices. Several months had passed and it was now May. Everything was bright and blooming. He had started his own large vegetable garden and his chickens and geese were thriving. He had purchased a rooster and he had named it Blaster. It ruled the roost and every morning Ken woke up to its shrill cries. He strutted around his little kingdom with pride and arrogance. Ken loved to watch him rule his domain. Ken was feeling quite contented but he didn't want close involvement with 'the Groups' if he could help it. The scars of the past reminded him to be wary. Ken went to town to purchase the goats. The goat farm was located just north of the town and as Ken headed towards it he hoped against hope that another group didn't own it.

His suspicions were aroused when he saw that all the buildings were painted yellow. He knew right away that the Yellow Group ran this place. As it was the only place to purchase goats, he breathed in deeply and decided to make a quick purchase and get out of there as fast as possible. He headed toward the yellow door of the yellow residence. Sure enough, there were several 'Yellows' there to greet him and they recognized him from the 'road rescue'! He tried to mumble some greetings and then tried to get down to business with them. Someone in the group looked at him closely and then he slapped Ken on the back and told him that he remembered him from Wonder! They are started laughing and recalling the good old days in Wonder. They regaled him with tales of camping outings on Black Mountain. Ken finally got them to take him to the goats and he picked out a pair, paid for them and then made a hasty retreat. He would have to stop dealing with these Groups but they seemed to run the agricultural aspect of the community. Would he ever escape his past?

Chapter Twenty-Two
Separation and Friendship

Ken determined that he'd separate himself from any association with the Groups. It was going to be difficult as they often tried to contact him. Ken hid when they stopped by his place. He didn't answer any suspicious-looking telephone calls. He began to feel isolated. He only went to town when he absolutely had to and then he scurried around completing his tasks and beat a retreat to his home. This was getting to be a strange way to live and Ken didn't see a way out as the community wasn't that large. He tried to get together with his town friends but that wasn't too often as they were busy working during the week. He concentrated on building his little "farm". He made a feeding trough for the goats. He decided to call them Billy and Sally and he hoped that they would have offspring soon. He worked long hours in his garden and on his grounds. It was looking very nice. However, he was lonely.

One day he was in town at the one and only grocery store buying much needed provisions when he thought that he spied Star's mother, Lily in the bakery section of the store. He slowly advanced closer and sure enough it was her but he didn't know if he should approach her or just leave the store hastily. That decision was taken from him as she turned and waved to him and then he had to talk to her. She told him that she was living in the town. She also informed him that Star was better now and was going to try and complete her studies and she hoped she'd be able to teach. Lily said that she hoped that Star would be able to get a job as close as possible to the town. Ken muttered some platitudes but he didn't tell her where he lived and then he left in a hurry. He didn't want to think about Star. She was in his past. The truth was that Lily really didn't know what was going on in her daughter's life.

When he got back to his place there was a message on his phone left by one of the Yellow Group's members informing him that the goats needed to have vaccinations. There was some kind of virus affecting their herd and they thought that it would be prudent to get his goats vaccinated as soon as possible. Ken groaned inwardly. He might meet some of them at the vet's and that is not what he wanted to happen at all. He decided that he'd get the job done as fast as possible and so he loaded the goats into his truck and headed for town again. They were easily spooked and so he drove slowly into town. When he got to the vet's he noticed quite a few trucks parked in front of the long white animal hospital. He just knew that he'd meet some of THEM. Sure enough, there were jovial laughs and slaps on the shoulder awaiting him as he ventured into the building with his reluctant goats. The Yellows were there in full force. Ken had to wait in the waiting room and before long, the Yellows were inviting him to a summer festival. They told him that there would be demonstrations about how to make goat cheese and yogurt. They suggested that Ken get into this business. Ken was interested but he didn't want to encourage them and so he muttered and nodded as they talked to him.

After the goats had received their shots they were very skittish and Ken had to calm them down before he could get them into his truck. It was late in the afternoon when he finally arrived back at his place. On his doorstep he found some beautiful flowers and some garden vegetables and he knew before he looked at the card that they were from his neighbours. The note said that they hoped that all was going well with him and there was an invitation to supper the next day. How could he get out of such a kind, neighbourly gesture? As he was feeling lonely he decided that he'd go and then not see them again for a very long time. Little did he realize that in this community it was very difficult to be isolated for very long.

The next evening Ken went to the Red Group's farm. They welcomed him with open arms as if he were a long lost son. The long table had flowers decorating it and everyone was seated and ready to eat. Ken sheepishly took his place near the end of the table. He was seated by a young lady with yellow hair and deep blue, laughing eyes. Her name was Daisy and he pictured her with a daisy chain in her hair. He didn't know where that idea had come from but there it was and he blushed. He hoped no one noticed but of course some of the younger children across the table looked at each other and giggled. Joseph Rodin was on the other side of him and he soon learned that Daisy was his sister. They all chattered together as the meal progressed. He found them to be great company. They all loved the outdoors and farming and so they had many things in common. Daisy said that she knew how to make goat cheese. The Reds were all going to the summer festival and they invited Ken to come too. Ken was not feeling as lonely after he had enjoyed an evening with this Group. He had to admit to himself that he had had a very enjoyable time with them. He mulled over as to whether he would go to the festival.

As the day of the festival loomed, Ken felt himself drawn to it. After all he could leave if he didn't like it and no one would stop him. The whole town was wound up about it. The streets were decorated with big banners. There was even going to be a parade. Ken gave up and decided to check this festivity out and try to enjoy it. It was on a Saturday and so Ken got up early so that he could see the parade. He got to the town in time to eat a free pancake breakfast. The streets were closed and everyone ate at tables on Main Street. A lot of people waved to him and Ken felt a sense of belonging.

He saw Daisy and Joseph and they decided to stick together for a while and look at some of the local displays. Ken was quite impressed by the array of skills that were represented. Then the parade started to come by on the next street. Everyone rushed to find a good viewing place. Daisy and Joseph were going to be on the Reds' float. They invited Ken to hop on it but he declined. He still wanted to keep some distance between them and himself. The parade turned out to be a representation of the Groups and other community interest groups. Ken wondered what kind of community this was and he thought to himself that unfortunately it was a lot like Wonder. Would he ever be able to get away from Groups? The floats were cleverly decorated and well-received by the crowd. There seemed to be little division today. Free samples of homemade products were thrown into the crowd. Ken was able to catch a knitted scarf from the Red float. It was red of course.

The rest of the day was spent looking at displays set up in a field at the edge of town. There was also a little rodeo for children. They were roping sheep. Ruth and John suddenly appeared in front of him in the crowd and they ate supper together on a picnic bench near the food section. They caught up on news and John warned that the 'dangerous' part of the day was going to come and Ken wondered what he was referring to but he didn't comment. As the sun made its descent down behind the hills, the mood changed. Everything went very quiet. The Groups suddenly appeared together in their colors and made circles and they all looked towards the setting sun. John nudged Ken as if to warn him about what was coming next. The Groups all stood a still as statues. When the sun went down they all erupted into cheers and ran toward the ridge. Ken was shocked. What were they going to do? They all tore up the sides of the hills and all who were left were the non-groups people staring at them. Apparently this was an annual ritual. Ruth said that they would all disappear over the ridge. She told Ken to wait to see what would happen next. Suddenly, the whole ridge was ablaze with fire. All the people were carrying torches and whooping and hollering. John said that this would last all night and he asked Ken if they could stay at his farm for the night as they would get no sleep if they stayed in town. Ken had seen enough. All three of them headed toward his place in his truck. Ken was peeved beyond words.

Chapter Twenty-Three
Puzzlement

Ken served his friends breakfast the next morning. They were in no hurry to head back to town as the groups would still be on the ridge causing problems for the town. Apparently they threw down rocks and yelled for hours on end. A lot of damage was usually done and then they would have to pay for it. Ken wanted to know what this was all about and he was informed that it was something to do with the middle of summer. Ken knew all about strange rituals and he was very troubled that he was again in the midst of turmoil. The Groups were so friendly but they had hidden agendas and he knew that he would have to be very careful around them in the future. He hated to have to have such a worry at the back of his mind while he lived in this community. His friends told him that they planned to move in a few months. They had had it with everything. Ken was unhappy to hear about this and he gloomily stared straight ahead as he drove them back to town. No one said anything. Everything seemed fairly hopeless.

Ken spent the rest of the summer on his little farm and painted pictures for the art show in Fernwood. His pictures were of rural farmland scenes with some of his farm scenes thrown in because there was a lot of subject material to paint on his own property. He felt satisfied with his efforts and loaded up his truck for the trip to Fernwood. He had asked a local farm boy (who didn't belong to a Group) to look after his livestock which now included one cow named Lizzy. He would be away for about three days. As he headed towards the city he mused as to whether he would have a successful show. It took several hours to get to Fernwood and it was evening when he arrived. He checked into a hotel and ate supper at its restaurant. As he was finishing up his dessert and sipping his coffee he noticed someone nearby who looked familiar. There was a middle-aged man sitting at the table opposite him and he was talking to two young men. They were having a very animated conversation. Ken could just make out a few words and it seemed that they were talking about a mountain and caves and a rally. Ken started to put things together in his mind and then he knew who these people were and he hunched into the corner of his booth to avoid being discovered. The older man was getting red in the face and the young men were gesturing with their hands and their voices were getting louder. People in the restaurant were starting to stare at them. Suddenly they all got up and left abruptly.

Ken was shaking in his booth. He hoped that they hadn't seen him. He was sure that the man was the Professor and the young men were probably University students. Were they planning new "activities" and who were they planning to terrorize and where would they be located? Quickly Ken slipped out of his booth and paid his bill and then he headed toward the parking lot to see if he could catch sight of the men. He saw them still talking loudly by a van. Ken's blood ran cold as he heard one of them say that they were headed to Deep Valley! The older man waved to the young men and he headed off into the darkness. Ken had heard enough! He surmised that the students were going to come to Deep Valley to start up another "colony". Why could he never get rid of them?

Ken could hardly focus on smiling politely to the many people who came to his art show in a local gallery on the following day. His pictures were well received and he sold nearly all of them quite quickly. He would be able to live quite comfortably for a long while on the sales he made that day. Although he should have been overjoyed at the success of his show, he wasn't. He just wanted to leave the city and head back to his farm and think about what to do with the rest of his life. He was puzzled, bewildered and totally confused. Why did these strange people seem to 'follow' him everywhere?

When Ken got back home he was exhausted. He rested for a while and then went out to check on his livestock. Everything seemed to be in order. As he was turning to go back to his house he saw some smoke ascending from the trees at the southern end of his property. He thought that was strange because no one lived in that area. He got out his binoculars and what he saw made him almost drop them. Several tents were on the edge of his property in fact, they seemed to be on his property. Who was squatting on his land? He decided he had to confront them. He started walking towards the tents. As he got nearer he recognized the two young men from the restaurant in Fernwood! He also noticed that their tents were definitely on his property. He informed them that they would have to move on as they were on his land. He also told them that camping was not allowed on other people's properties. The young men stared and him and then politely told him that they'd leave the next day. Ken went back to his house and sat down with his head in his hands at his kitchen table. Gradually, as he thought over these recent events, he began to see that he needed to get away from this place. He thought about *really* getting away and that would mean to another country. Maybe a long vacation would help him to assess his life.

    Ken quickly put plans together so that he could leave his farm for about a month. He had decided that he'd go to Australia and that two local farm boys could oversee his property and animals. He sadly had to give away his precious pets. He harvested his garden and froze vegetables. One of the boys would check on his house every day. Ken looked up information on walking treks or tours in the Australian Outback. Surely no strange groups would be there! The tent people had left and Ken hoped that they wouldn't return - ever. Ken was now ready for an adventure.

Chapter Twenty-Four
Mountains Brought Low

Ken flew to Sydney, Australia the next week. He was glad to get far away from his farm. He had to clear his head and set his life in a new direction. He didn't have the faintest clue as to how to achieve a new life. He spent several days in Sydney seeing the sights and enjoying having no particular schedule. He inquired about various treks in the Outback at the hotel where he was staying and he found that he could fly there the next day and be ready to join a party which would set out in two days. He quickly bought some outdoor clothes and he flew out the next day, ready to begin to explore this special land. He was intrigued by the landscapes below as he neared his destination. Central Australia looked barren but Ken was sure that once he landed he'd find adventures awaiting him. He was going to go on a trek to Ayers Rock. There would be only eight people on the trip including himself and the guide who was also the driver.

He was met at his hotel by the guide and he soon was introduced to his fellow travelers. They were all about his age and they soon were laughing together as if they had known each other all their lives. The guide spent a lot of time with them teaching them about the environment and what to expect on the trip. Ken was excited and he couldn't sleep the night before he was to set out on his Outback experience. He had already become more cheerful and he looked forward to the trek out into the wilderness and away from the strange people he always seemed to be around where he lived. He was ready to enjoy every bit of his adventure. All thoughts of home were obliterated as he looked forward to finding out about this fascinating place.

At the crack of dawn the eager travelers piled into the van and they were soon headed toward their adventures in the Outback. They ate a camp-type breakfast about an hour later as the sun beat down on them. Their guide had been informing them about the points of interest they would encounter that day and Ken was looking forward to taking a lot of pictures. He wanted to paint some scenes when he got back home. He was also learning many new Australian expressions and slang words. As they bumped along on the dusty orange road they all sang Australian bush songs amidst much laughter at each other's musical abilities. One of the campers had a guitar which helped a lot. Ken couldn't sing very well but he pretended to make some "musical noise". They were headed towards Ayers Rock and Ken was eager to see this landmark. He had always been puzzled ever since his "Wonder" experiences about why people wanted to go to prominent landscapes and why they were so special. It seemed that since his arrival at that strange village, he had witnessed mad scrambles for high hills or mountains. He had read about the history of Ayers Rock and as it loomed on the horizon in all its orange glory, Ken felt his curiosity increase as he peered at it through the dust and heat.

The happy travelers piled out of the van and their guide assembled the little group around him and told them about where they were allowed to go and what not to do on the Rock. The environment had to be protected and therefore there were strict rules as to where they were allowed to tread. Ken was glad when it was announced that they would eat first before ascending the Rock. He was very hungry and thirsty. They ate under a tarp and enjoyed the sandwiches and cold juice that was provided. It was great "tucker". He had enjoyed the snags (sausages) the best. Everyone got their water bottles filled and adjusted their hats and light gear and set off. Ken followed right behind the guide and listened to every word he said as they toiled up the side to the Rock. The higher they got the farther Ken could see the vast plain around the Rock spreading out in all directions. There were a lot of scrubby plants and some tall trees nearer to the Rock. Ayers Rock was also known as Uluru and it was a monolith that rose from the land and seemed like a lump of red clay. It was all so strange. Ken felt like he was on another planet. This "mountain" was special to the Aborigines just like other mountains Ken could name but he didn't want to think about them at this time. He viewed the vastness of the land before him and he felt that he would like to explore more of this fascinating country. Unfortunately he had to think about going home as he needed to check up on his place. He mused about owning a ranch somewhere in Australia. He was brought back from his thoughts when it was announced that they would be descending and then they would have a light supper before heading back to town.

Everyone had enjoyed the trek up the Rock and there was a lot of chatter about it. They all seemed to have enjoyed the day's outing but they were tired. As they bumped along the dusty road to town most of them were sleeping. Ken sat in his seat and stared out at the passing views and he decided that he would definitely come back again. He then felt sleepy and he soon joined the others in dreamland.

Ken felt increasing urgency about the need to return to his farm. He decided that he'd leave sooner than he had planned and the next day Ken was on a plane to Sydney and then he connected to a flight to head home. He had promised to keep in contact with some of the people he had met on his trip. He grew increasingly anxious as he got nearer to his home. After traveling many miles he finally arrived at his own front gate. However, the gate was not there! Something was wrong! As he approached his front door he noticed that some of the windows on his house were broken. He walked around the house and to his horror he saw that all of his animals were GONE! He was trembling as he fiddled with the key to the back door. What met his eyes was terrible but all too familiar. His place had been ransacked and had been used by those who didn't care about his property. So much for the help he thought he had had all this time. In short, his place was unlivable and destroyed! Ken buried his head in his hands and cried. This had happened far too often to him and he couldn't take it anymore. He sat on his back step for a long time and wondered what he was going to do next. He informed the local police force but he didn't hold out too much hope that the culprits would be caught.

Ken came to the realization that he was beat. He would have to move very far away from this place. But where? It seemed trouble was following him everywhere he went and he was becoming increasingly anxious and he seemed to be looking over his shoulder waiting for the next disaster to occur. This was no way to live. Ken then sprang into action. He would move so far away that no one would know where he was and he would be able to lead a peaceful and safe life. He worked hard over the next few days to bring some order out of the chaos. He then was able to sell the house and land quite quickly (which went very cheaply) and soon he was packed and ready to leave this horrible place. He informed Ellie that she could have his home outside of Wonder and that she could take over the responsibilities for the apartments. He knew where he was going to go and he could hardly wait to start a brand new life.

Chapter Twenty-Five
A Fresh Start

Ken had decided that he would move to a place where he had often wanted to live and never thought he'd be able to go to because of the distance and the events that were taking place in his life. Now he was more or less free to go wherever he so desired. He was going to go to Switzerland! He wanted to go to a village and paint and do whatever he pleased without being constantly on edge as to what would happen next. He headed for Monza to settle his art contracts with the gallery and to sell his truck. He spent some time in a travel agency asking questions. He had to stay in Monza for a week to wait for his passport to arrive.

Ken decided that he would travel lightly and acquire what he needed in Switzerland. He would be a permanent resident there for many years, he hoped. One morning, as he sipped his coffee in his hotel's restaurant, he looked up as he heard a commotion near the till. A rather large lady was arguing about her bill and everyone in the restaurant was staring at her antics. The cashier was trying to reason with her but to no avail. Ken looked carefully at the cashier and he almost fell off his chair when he realized that it was Star! The woman was starting to hurl threats and was totally out of control. Ken rushed towards Star and as she looked up at him in astonishment, Ken shouted for her to call security. In a few minutes two large men in dark uniforms had the lady by the arms and were ushering her out of the restaurant. She could be heard screaming as they put her into a patrol car.

Star was shaken and she was relieved by another girl at the till. Ken invited her to his table. Star sat quietly and stared at Ken. Ken didn't know what to say to her but he attempted a few platitudes about the situation. After a few minutes she started to talk. What she had to say caused Ken to sit up and listen intently. Star told Ken that her life was a mess. Shortly after her release from the hospital she had married one of the men from the crazy group she had been associated with and her life became a living hell. He was forever taking off on "adventures" and taking all their money with him which left Star destitute. One day he didn't return and it was discovered that he had died in an avalanche on a mountain he was trying to "conquer". Star's dreams of becoming a teacher had been dashed and she had to find work. She was currently working at three jobs and hoping to be able to save money towards completing her education. Star continued on to inform Ken that she had dropped any further association with the "crazies". She was thankful for being alive but her life was terribly hard and lonely. She didn't want her Mother to know how hard her life was and that she had told her lies about her real life. That was why she didn't communicate with her very much. Ken mentioned that he had met her Mother and that she believed all was well with her daughter. Star tearfully told Ken that she'd never tell her Mother about her real life.

Ken felt terribly sorry for Star. Her life had held such promise. He didn't tell her all about his artistic successes and that he was independently wealthy. All he did tell her was that he was leaving the country but that he would like to be able to contact her and so she gave him her address. Ken looked at her pale, thin face and wished that he could help her and make things better. She was too proud to accept money, he knew. He didn't know how to help her and that made him feel frustrated. She knew that he was a successful artist because she had seen his work in the gallery. Ken gave her a hug and watched her slowly walk away towards the till. She was so thin and almost lifeless. What a life!

Ken flew to Zurich the next day and booked into the nearest hotel. It would be his headquarters until he found the right place. It was going to be winter in a few months and he needed to be settled before the snow fell. He arranged to go on a bus tour of several small towns and villages and then he planned to pick the town or village he liked the best and then he would buy his home. He was very excited. He could hardly sleep that night in his hotel room. The beginning of a life free from strange intruders and kooks would be so great!

Ken thoroughly enjoyed his trip the next day. It was such a beautiful country! He was able to converse with most of the people he met because he could speak German fairly well. Their German was a little different but he could make out what they were describing. He wanted to live in a small town near the mountains. He didn't think that anyone from some "cult" would be living in a small town in Switzerland. The last town he visited was so charming. He was able to inquire about chalets for sale. Sure enough, there was one at the foot of a tall mountain ready for immediate occupancy. Ken went to look at it and knew that it was "his place". He sealed the sale that day. He would be able to move into it in a week.

Ken scoured local furniture stores for basics and bought cooking supplies and linens. He enjoyed the charming shops and the atmosphere was so relaxed and friendly. He was beginning to feel really at home. These items would be delivered to his new place. Ken was able to sample the food of his newly adopted country and he knew that he was going to enjoy everything it had to offer in the culinary sense. Cheeses and chocolates of the highest quality and variety abounded. He was beginning to relax and not look over his shoulder every two minutes. He found himself laughing with shop keepers and waiters. This was truly going to be a great new beginning. However, he was in for some disturbing surprises.

Ken moved into his three bedroom chalet and started to arrange his new furniture in it. What was missing? Oh yes! He needed a cat or two and perhaps a dog. He introduced himself to the nearest neighbor and found out that she had a cat that had just given birth to seven kittens! He chose two kittens, one a female and the other a male. He named them Hope and Happy. They would be the symbols of his new life. The lady's name was Maria and she lived alone in a small house about half a kilometer away from Ken. She was a retired seamstress and she seemed so nice. Surely, nothing could be strange about her or her home! Ken mused to himself about how fortunate he was to have such a great neighbor.

Chapter Twenty-Six
Winter Wonderland

Soon after Ken moved in it began to snow. Great fluffy flakes fell softly to the ground. Soon the landscape was covered with a white blanket. Ken thought it looked so beautiful. It was so quiet and peaceful. He felt he was alone on a perfect planet. He wished that he had a dog to play with in the snow. He decided to visit Maria and ask her if she knew where he could find a dog. He missed Orie so much! He set off at once enjoying the cool moisture and watching the falling snow. He arrived at Maria's place and knocked on her back door. He could hear voices inside and he realized that she had visitors.

Maria opened the door and smiled broadly at Ken. She ushered him into her cozy kitchen and thrust a large cup of coffee in a blue mug into his hand as he sat down at her kitchen table. Ken looked into the little sitting room and saw two men talking softly to each other on the couch. Maria told Ken that they were friends from town and that they had been discussing some business. Ken waved to them and they waved back and kept on talking in an earnest manner. Ken wondered why they didn't join him and Maria in the kitchen.

Maria had just baked a coffee cake and she offered Ken a generous slice which Ken quickly set in to demolish. In between bites and swallows he talked to Maria and asked her where he could find a dog. She suggested that he put up an ad on the town bulletin board and see if anyone answered it. Ken said that was a good idea and he asked her to write out in German what to say on the ad. She took a piece of paper from a drawer and the two of them came up with what they thought was a great advertisement. They chatted about the snow and about what winters were like there and then Ken bid her adieu (with another wave to the chatting men) and set off for his home.

As he trudged home in the snow (which was piling up all around him), Ken couldn't get the men out of his mind. What were they really at Maria's for and was she in any danger? He decided to check on her again later in the day. After a light lunch Ken decided that he needed a small truck to get around with and so he set out for town to see if he could find such a vehicle. Luckily there was a dealership on the edge of town and he was soon looking over the inventory. He found a small red truck that was perfect for his needs and he bought it and jumped into it and drove around town looking for the town bulletin board. He found it near a small food store and put the ad on it. He placed it squarely in the middle of the bulletin board.

As he chugged home in his new truck he looked up at the towering mountains all around and wondered at their height. They were getting covered in the falling snow. Soon the ski hills would open and Ken had already signed up for ski lessons. He could hardly wait to go tearing down a ski trail. Then he checked himself and realized that he'd have to practice a lot first before he tore down a steep mountainside! Ken realized that he should have purchased a snow shovel as he could hardly get into his driveway. After a rest he started out for Maria's again. He arrived to find everything silent. There were no voices and after knocking on the door and even the windows, he got no response. He went to the front of her house and noticed relatively fresh car tracks which had backed out of the driveway. What concerned Ken was that it appeared that someone had fallen in the snow and the others had been around that person either to help them up or push them down! Ken noticed smaller footprints leading away from the area where someone had "fallen" and two sets of larger footprints joining them and all of them leading to the vehicle. Ken was now afraid for Maria's safety. He saw that the front door hadn't been tightly closed and so he opened it up and peered inside. What he saw caused him to become very terrified.

Chapter Twenty-Seven
Missing Maria

Ken turned on a light and saw that the whole sitting room was turned upside down. Furniture was knocked down, drawers were open, china was scattered on the floor and signs of a struggle were everywhere. In the kitchen similar evidence of a rampage was discovered. Those men had torn her house apart and had taken her! Why? She wouldn't harm a flea. Ken didn't know any of her friends and so he decided that he'd have to contact the local police. Ken felt that he was reliving what he'd done many times before in a different land. He so wished this wasn't happening again. He called the police from Maria's phone in her kitchen. He waited for them to arrive and when they did he explained everything he knew. They started their investigation right away and told him to be available for further questioning. He trudged away to his house with his head down and his steps slow and shuffling. What had happened?

Ken called the police the next day and they told him that they had no leads and that Maria's property was off limits. Over the next few weeks there was sporadic activity on Maria's property but after that there was nothing. No one came and the house was boarded up and it looked so lonely and deserted that Ken didn't want to come near the property. The police had no clues. It was as if Maria had been lifted off the planet.

Ken started his ski lessons and tried to keep his mind off of Maria's disappearance. He really enjoyed his lessons and he was soon promoted to the intermediate class. After a month of practice and instruction he was able to ski down a moderate slope without too many falls. He met some new friends and soon they were all skiing together every chance they got and that was usually on the weekends. After skiing they enjoyed lunch or supper together at the chalet restaurant at the bottom of the ski hill. His friends were Canadians who were working in town for the experience. They came from western Canada and were used to skiing. They were Brian and Jim and they had been friends since childhood. Ken invited them to his house and he cooked super meals for them all and they had great times together. He talked to them about his neighbor but they hadn't known her and they all mused together as to where she might be and if she was still alive. It was a black cloud over Ken's life but he tried to push it aside. What could he do about it?

Chapter Twenty-Eight
A Surprise

Ken wanted to do something for Star and so he invited her to come for Christmas. She said that it was impossible but thanked him for the invitation. Ken was downhearted but hoped that he could persuade her to come in the Spring. He sent a huge parcel to her filled with Swiss delicacies and souvenirs. Ken invited his friends to spend Christmas day with him. They planned to ski the next day. After stuffing themselves with turkey they wanted to get some exercise and so they all set out to conquer the nearest highest mountain and to be able to swoop down from its heights. It was a bright, crisp day as they rode the gondola to the peak. They were amazed at how far they could see and were eagerly awaiting their arrival at the top. There were two other men were in the gondola. They said that they were American tourists and that they had skied down this mountain before and they promised a great skiing experience. Ken felt that these men were men he had met before but he couldn't remember where he had met them. He pushed those thoughts from his mind as he jumped out of the gondola. The Americans said that they were going for a snowshoe trek on the mountain and they waved goodbye. Ken felt that was a little odd but he got ready for his great adventure.

After several runs down the mountain Ken was exhausted. He looked for the men but he saw no one. As he waited for the gondola with his friends he saw a flash of light out of the corner of his eye. It seemed to flash a few times. Ken felt that he was getting over-anxious about nothing. He saw nothing on the mountain. He also thought he heard a high pitched sound far away but he couldn't determine if it was an animal or human sound. Ken felt that something was amiss but he couldn't really determine if he was imagining it or not and so he left the mountain with his friends. They didn't see the Americans.

Ken went about painting and he explored his new surroundings. He had tried to hard to find peace but even here in Switzerland he felt an emptiness. He felt somewhat purposeless. He was going to have a showing of his current works of art at a local art gallery. He kept busy finishing up his pieces. He took photos of local landmarks. He went up the gondola to take pictures of the mountain area where he had skied with his friends. He trudged further up the mountain to get a few unusual shots. As he passed a forested area he was surprised to hear voices! There seemed to be a small group in the woods. Ken was surprised to find people this far up the mountain. Ken hid behind a rock and watched the area and soon he was astonished to see the two Americans emerge with a middle-aged woman. It was Maria! Ken was sure of it! She was struggling and fighting them. What could he do for her without being discovered himself?

Chapter Twenty-Nine
A Long Wait

Ken shivered behind the rock. They were coming closer! He could now hear what they were saying to one another. They were disputing about money. He heard the words, "mission" and "family". What was this all about? Ken noticed that the sun was gone and that it was getting darker and colder. They seemed to be trying to drag Maria towards the gondola but she was resisting. Ken now realized that the men were the same men he had encountered in her home. He hadn't really looked closely at them when he was visiting with Maria. Why did they want money? Was it her money that they were trying to get access to and for what reason? Maria sat down in the snow crying and it was all that Ken do to keep from jumping on the men. Luckily Ken had his cell phone and he retreated silently from his place near the rock to get some distance between them and himself. He dialed for help from the police. He was fortunate that he was able to contact them. Now he had to wait it out on that cold, dark mountain. The men had dragged Maria back into the forested area and he could hear her crying for help. Soon he saw a fire in the forest and all was relatively quiet. Ken shivered and wondered how long it would be for the police to arrive. He was getting tired and he was hungry. Finally after an hour he heard the gondola ascending. Ken was ready and watching.

The police rushed out of the gondola with three search dogs eager to get started in finding their "prey". Ken emerged from his hiding place and pointed in the direction of where the captors and captive were hidden. However, he noticed that there was no fire and all was very silent. Where were they? The police team fanned out and Ken was ordered to wait behind his rock. Ken listened and watched as they all disappeared into the forest. All he heard were muffled voices and barking dogs. After about half an hour they all came straggling back but they had not caught anyone! The police were baffled. The cold ashes of the fire had been located and they had followed footprints in the snow and then the dogs lost their scent. It seemed that they had vanished! Their next plan was to leave two men on the mountain overnight and then relieve them the next day with two more men. These men would conduct searches while on duty. Ken had to get off the mountain as he was totally exhausted. He rode down the mountain in the gondola with the police and their dogs. They all were perplexed.

The next day Ken decided to go up the mountain again and try to search with the police. He went on a patrol with them. The snow was undisturbed after about ten meters from the fire. He looked around carefully and then he saw a glint of light flashing ahead of him. It seemed to be on the surface of a rocky ridge. He cautiously approached it and noticed the light dancing around on it. The other policemen were searching elsewhere. He looked in the direction from which he thought that the light might be coming from and to his horror he caught a glimpse of an opening in the rock face and he heard muffled noises. He inched closer to the opening. He peered carefully into it and he could just pick out the forms of people around a light. They were arguing and there was a pushing match going on between them. Ken planned to get back to the policemen to get their help but suddenly an arm reached around the opening and grabbed Ken by his collar! Then his mouth was covered by a hand and he was dragged into the cavern.

Chapter Thirty
Mysterious Messages

Ken kicked and tried to punch his assailant but to no avail. He was dragged into the cave and hauled up in front of another man and Maria! Maria cried when she saw him. She mumbled about how sorry she was that he had got caught into all of this craziness. Maria looked totally hopeless and scared. The men tied him up and made him sit on the cold stone floor of the cave. The men were arguing about who was going to go and get food and water. Their provisions had run out. Finally one of them stumbled out of the cave. Ken hoped that he would get caught by the police. Maria sat next to him and tried to explain in a whisper about what this was all about and how she had become mixed up in it. The other man stood by with the flashlight and stared sullenly at them.

These men had come to her home and told her that they were related to her and that she had to come to a nearby town to claim money from the will of a recently dead Uncle. She had resisted them and they had dragged her away to this mountain. They had been living in this cave ever since. There had been a lot of provisions but now they were gone and the men were panicking and getting violent. Maria had tried to send messages by using her glasses as a reflector in the hope of attracting attention. Maria couldn't figure out what they wanted except her money that she had in a bank account in Zurich. She had been able to save a sizeable amount of money over the years. They had told her that they had a mission on the mountain and other people were coming to set up a colony there in the near future. They told her that she would enjoy being a part of such a great group of people and that she would be the mother of them all if she would agree to give them her money. Of course Maria thought that they were crazy and had resisted them up until this point. Now she was beginning to feel like giving up. Ken admonished her to stay strong. He told her that the police knew about these men and that they would get caught. The man by the light told them to shut up and then he said it was time to read the messages. Ken was puzzled. Maria nudged him as if to say that he should wait and see what happened next.

He pushed them toward the back of the cave and shone his light on the wall. On it were messages written in a spidery-like scrawl. They were all about the mountain and how special it was and that it would be the center of the Universe soon. It needed people devoted to setting up a colony to wait for the end of the world. Ken inwardly laughed. Maria winked at him. These men believed this stuff! The man told them that he and his pal had discovered these "sacred writings" while they had been snowshoeing around the area. They had heard in town that Maria was a "saver" and that she had a lot of money stashed away in a Zurich Bank. Their plan began to form.

Of course Ken had heard all this before in different places from different people who had all been looking for "salvation" from a high mountainous area. Was this a world-wide phenomenon? Why was he always mixed up in their schemes? Ken sighed and thought about what he could do next to manage an escape for himself and Maria. Then he thought of a plan.

Ken decided that he would pretend to have an attack of appendicitis. If he could get down the mountain by some chance, he could get help. His cell phone had been taken by the men and so he had come up with this plan. He began to groan and grab his side. The man told him to be quiet and stop his whimpering. Ken started to writhe on the floor of the cave. Maria was trying to help Ken but she didn't know what to do and so she begged the man to do something. The man asked him what he was hollering about and he muttered that his side hurt. Ken kept saying that he thought it might be appendicitis. Maria cried out that he needed help right away! The man pushed her away and told Ken to get out as he couldn't stand the yelping any longer. Maria asked to help him but the man ignored her and pushed Ken outside. Ken couldn't believe his luck. He hoped that he wouldn't run into the other man coming back to the cave.

Ken crept toward the edge of the forest and eyed the gondola. Unfortunately the other man was emerging from it with a load of groceries and supplies. He even had purchased a sled and he piled it high and started to set forth towards the cave and Ken! Where were the police when he needed them? How had that man got back and forth on the gondola without meeting any of them? What was going on? The answer to that question came none too soon. He noticed a form lying on the other side of the gondola in the snow. It was a body! He glanced all around the area and he found another body! That man had shot them! Ken was in great danger and so was Maria! These were dangerous men! Ken hoped that more police would appear soon but it was still early in the day and the night shift wouldn't be on duty for a while. Ken decided to hang around to see what would occur. He didn't want to get shot entering the gondola. He couldn't call for help as he didn't have his cell phone.

Ken saw the man disappear into the forest with his sled. All was quiet. It was a sunny day. Not even a bird sang and no noise made Ken jumpy. He did hear some faint noises from the cave area and he worried about Maria. After an hour Ken emerged from his hiding place and dashed for the gondola. He hoped that he could get down the mountain safely.

Chapter Thirty-One
Rescue

Ken was able to get down from the mountain and to get the police up on the mountain again. He joined them as he wanted to make sure Maria was safely brought down the mountain. The police had supplied extra men and now the cave was surrounded. They had warned the men to let Maria go free or else they would have to storm the cave. There was no reply. After about half an hour the cave was entered to find - nothing and no one there at all! Ken was puzzled. They had absolutely cleaned up everything and there was no evidence that anyone had been inhabiting the cave. The police sent dogs to sniff out the area. The dogs were excited by something at the back of the cave. After careful inspection they found that there was a way to enter another part of the cave. After trying to open up a crack in the wall they were finally successful and they were able to enter another room of the cave. There huddled in the shadows was Maria! Where were the men? Maria was hysterical with relief. She threw herself into Ken's arms and cried uncontrollably. Finally, after a while she was calm enough to tell them about what had happened.

The men had become nervous because Ken had been allowed to go free. There had been a huge fight between the men about Ken's release. It was decided that they should leave and put Maria into the other room. Maria had been in the dark for several hours. She had been terrified. All she could envision was herself starving to death in that terrible place. The police immediately sent their dogs outside to find the culprits. They couldn't have gone too far. However, all that they found were some scattered provisions. There was a trail of food and garbage. The dogs sniffed the gondola and got excited. It was then clear that the men had got away!

Sentries were posted on the mountain. The dead bodies of the policemen and all the rest of them were piled into the gondola and they headed back to civilization. Maria stayed at Ken's place until she decided what to do next. She was quite shaken and Ken wanted her to get some professional help to help her deal with the trauma she had been subjected to for such a long time. She was stubborn about this and so Ken let it alone. After a week Maria had decided to move away to Zurich. Her house was put up for sale and preparations were made for her belongings to be moved to Zurich. Ken helped her pack and soon, before he knew it, she was gone and Ken was left wondering what would happen to her and what he would do next.

Chapter Thirty-Two
Success

Ken had his art show and he had become a hero in the town. His part in the rescue was splashed across the headlines in several major newspapers. He got into media news. He was asked for an interview by an American news network but he declined. He was mistrustful about who these men had been connected to and he didn't want to give out any more information about himself. His art show had sold out and Ken felt very pleased. He was getting known as an artist in Switzerland. Orders started piling in for his paintings of local sights.

The men had not been found. Ken felt very uneasy about that and that kept him on edge. He finally went up the mountain about three months later. It was late spring and there was little snow and no one appeared to be around. He went toward the cave and he noticed muddy footprints around the entrance. Who had been there? The police had given up their search and so the mountain did not have a police presence. He put his ear by the entrance to the cave and he thought he heard something. He told himself that this was impossible. Then to his surprise he saw someone coming toward the cave! He was just able to hide before he was discovered. It was a raggedly dressed woman with long hair. She yelled at the cave entrance and someone inside moved the big rock which was blocking the opening. Ken was petrified! It was happening again! People hiding in caves. People trying to reach some other "plain" of existence! Again he asked himself the question as to why he always got involved in these situations. His head was spinning. Here he was a successful artist and he was slinking around a cave on a mountain. He had done all this before and why did he always run into these kinds of people? Let them find their "answers". He was disgusted with himself. He rushed away to the gondola and vowed never to be mixed up with kooks again!

As Ken traveled slowly down the mountainside he began to reconsider his decision about leaving well enough alone. These people might cause others danger or be a danger to themselves. His past history with this "fringe element" had proved that they usually caused chaos and suffering. He mulled over about what he should do as he walked to the coffee shop at the gondola landing. As he was sipping his coffee he noticed an elderly man near him and he decided to ask him a rather unusual question. He didn't know why he felt that this man would listen to him. He looked benevolent and kindly. Ken asked if he could sit next to him and the man smiled and waved him to the seat.

Ken introduced himself and the man told him that he was the pastor of the church on the main street of the town. Ken was surprised but tried to hide his feelings. After a few pleasantries, Ken felt he could ask his question. He asked why people strive to find out the meaning of life by endangering themselves and others in their quest. The pastor, who wanted to be called Sean, told him that the quest was more important to them than any obstacle or impediment that got in the way. He reiterated the history about various cultures and the rituals and temples (often in high places or elevated in some manner) that had been built which often involved death and severe hardship. Ken fell silent for a while. He then felt safe enough to ask Sean if a citizen should report possible dangerous activities of a sect. Sean replied that it was always important to report anything that would harm fellow citizens. He would need some proof, if possible.

Ken told Sean that he knew about strange activities which might be occurring nearby. Sean looked interested. Taking the "bull by the horns", Ken told him about his own history and then he informed him about what was now occurring on the mountain above them. Sean marveled at all the situations that Ken had been involved in and then he told Ken that to have it happen again was Providential. Ken looked at him with a puzzled frown on his face. Did Sean think that God was trying to tell him something? Of course Sean would say that as he was a "religious" person. Ken was thinking thoughts along these lines when Sean asked if he could come with him to the place where these people were hiding. After a moment or two Ken decided that he'd let Sean see the cave. He had someone on his side.

The following morning the two new friends were on their way up the mountain. Ken had brought along his camera this time. Sean looked excited. His cheeks seemed even pinker against his light blue sweater and his round face was lit up under his white hair. Ken told Sean to be very careful and not make a sound. After a short trek they were in eyeshot of the cave. All was quiet. Then from the opening came five people. Ken took a picture of them. They all looked like they were dressed in burlap and to say the least, they were all very unkempt. There appeared to be three women and two men. They had pick axes and shovels and they headed up the mountain behind the cave. What were they up to? Ken and Sean followed them like stealthy tigers. Near the top of the mountain they saw them again. They were all hard at work trying to dig what looked like a big hole. Ken took another picture. He had successfully caught them in "the act". It was getting late and so the two "spies" quickly headed back to the gondola.

Chapter Thirty-Three
Strange Rituals

The two new friends enjoyed a late meal in a restaurant in town. Sean wanted to go again and look at what these people were doing in order to get a clearer picture of what was occurring on the mountain. He took Ken to his church and invited him to come to services if he so desired. Ken didn't really want to get involved in religion. However, he did say that he'd drop by to visit Sean from time to time if that was all right. Sean said that it would be fine. They planned to go up the mountain in a few days. Ken was hopeful that when he went to the police he would have sufficient documentation about the '"mountain activities".

Ken looked up information on the history of different people groups around the world and the religious rituals they were involved in and he was beginning to see that there was a thread of similarity in them. What struck him was the effort and sacrifice that went into the pursuit of finding meaning in this life and the life to come. He had seen that in all the groups he had been involved with and he wondered where their "passion" came from as he didn't seem to have IT. The high country or places such as caves or buildings made them feel closer to finding their answers. Maybe Sean could enlighten him about why people chose high altitudes to build their way up higher to reach what they thought they needed.

During the next week that followed Sean and Ken went exploring and spying on these strange people on the mountain. They had dug a huge circular hole and were beginning to lay down trees that they had cut for a floor of sorts. They had then rimmed it with large stones. The labour involved was extensive and it made Ken tired watching them struggle with few tools to achieve their dream - whatever that was…. When the circle was completed Sean and Ken witnessed the strangest "ritual". They all stood together holding hands around the perimeter of the circle. There were about a dozen of them - all young and dressed very shabbily. The men all had beards and the women all seemed to have long hair which was not styled in any particular fashion. They all howled like wolves and then fell silent and then they solemnly marched around the circle without a sound. After that they sat down and looked up at the sky with raised hands. They did this three times and then they left for the cave. Sean and Ken looked at each other and they too, left, silently.

Sean invited Ken to his place for supper and they discussed what they had witnessed. Other than logging the mountain and displacing rocks and ruining some plants, the group had not disturbed others. They were trespassing on Government land. Ken was so puzzled by what the group was doing around the circle. Sean said that he wasn't surprised because rituals were always involved in belief systems. Ken had to agree as he had seen many strange rituals over the years. Ken thought that they might be waiting for something to happen in the sky because the cave message seemed to imply that something was to occur in the heavens. Sean suggested that they continue to watch this group before going to the authorities. Maybe he could have contact with the group and try to find out what they hoped to accomplish on the mountain. Ken wasn't so sure about this plan but he reluctantly agreed to wait a while longer before informing the police. Ken was worried that the men would come back and join the group on the mountain. These men were armed and dangerous.

Chapter Thirty-Four
Encounter!

Ken and Sean set out early the next day with provisions and extra clothing. They struggled up the mountain and settled in to watch the circle. No one was there. It was getting quite boring staring at the ragged hole when suddenly the trees opposite them started to move and out of the forest came two men. Ken peered narrowly at them and was amazed and startled to discover that they were the two escaped men. Now Ken was really concerned. He stared at Sean who was watching them. Sean seemed calm. The escapees approached the circle and examined it carefully. They started cutting branches from the fir trees nearby and then they laid them in the center of the circle. What were they doing? Ken tried to warn Sean about the men by making strange faces and pointing to them. Sean looked puzzled. The two men then sat down in the center of the circle and yelled at the top of their lungs. After a few minutes of this ear-splitting noise, the members of the "cult" came silently from the forest and joined the men in the center of the circle.

They all moved like zombies in a silent, awkward manner. They stood and then sat down and then they repeated this "exercise" two more times. Sean was getting restless. Ken felt that Sean wanted to talk to them. Ken frowned at him and motioned to him to sit still and not talk. The two criminals stood up in front of the group and started yelling at them for not getting things done properly. Apparently the circle wasn't up to their standards. One young man ventured to suggest that they hadn't much food and that they were getting weaker. One of the men hit him and that silenced the young man who fell down and started to sob. Then others started to cry and wail. The men were beside themselves with anger and then one of them shot once in the air with his gun and silence returned to the unhappy group.

Sean stood up and to Ken's horror, advanced toward the group! Ken tried to grab him but Sean eluded his grasp and emerged from their hiding place and headed toward the group! The men pointed guns at him. Ken decided that he'd keep out of the way as now he would definitely have to contact the authorities. He had a cell phone and he planned to use it.

Sean went toward the group with his hands raised and smiled at them and said that he had come as a friend. He told them who he was and that he knew that they needed help. The two men growled at him to be quiet and to get down on his knees. They demanded to know how he knew that they were there and what he was there for and how could he help them. Ken had seen enough. He edged back into the forest and used his cell phone to quietly inform the police about the situation.

When he got back to his hiding place, Sean was standing up and talking quietly to the group and they were all listening attentively, including the two ringleaders! He had somehow convinced them that he was harmless and they listened respectfully to him! Ken heard Sean tell them that he understood their quest and that he was there to help them and not harm them. Ken gulped. Now what? The police were on their way and what would happen to them all, including himself and Sean? Sean told them that he had some provisions and clothing for them. He told them that he wanted to understand what they believed was supposed to happen on this mountain. Ken decided that he'd better move far away from the circle. He left the food and water that they had brought. He felt like a coward as he headed toward the gondola. He thought he would be a better help to Sean and the others if he was there to greet the police and show them where the action was taking place.

Finally, after what seemed ages, the police came and Ken led them to the mountain top. When they got there, Ken was horrified to see that not a soul was there at all! All the footprints were there but not a human being was to be found. The food and water were gone. Where was Sean? Ken was torn with guilt. Why had he involved this good man in such an evil situation?

Chapter Thirty-Five
Surrender

Ken led the police to the cave because he thought that Sean and the group would probably be in it. They ringed the cave waiting for a showdown. The group was told to come out with their hands raised. One of the men shouted out from the opening. He told them that Sean was now their hostage and he would come to harm if they were forced to come out of the cave. The police Captain informed them that force would be necessary if they didn't come out at once. A few moments of silence followed. Then a dingy sheet was waved out of the gap beside the stone door. The rock was moved and the group filed out one by one. The two men came and then last of all, Sean appeared! He smiled at Ken and Ken ran toward him and hugged him tightly. The group was rounded up and no one got away this time. Ken and Sean straggled along and arrived at Sean's house at midnight. What a day! As they were exhausted and hungry, they ate a big meal and then Ken fell asleep on Sean's couch.

The next morning was Sunday. Sean had to get ready for the church service. Ken decided to stay and attend it. He enjoyed the quiet dignity of the worship and he felt at peace. Sean spoke about forgiveness and also grace. Ken couldn't quite understand it all but it felt good to sit there and listen to Sean's quiet and steady voice. The small choir sang a wonderful song about God's unchanging love and Ken felt peaceful and saw the future as being more hopeful somehow. He only remembered one verse from Sean's sermon and it was from the Psalms. It was Psalms 97:9. It said that the LORD was "high above all the earth: (and that He was) exalted far above all gods." At least these people didn't need to climb to high places to achieve happiness. He wished that he had their faith but it was nice to feel it radiating from them. After the service Ken stood near Sean at the door of the church as Sean greeted the people as they left to go to their homes.

Sean and Ken had a simple lunch together at a local cafe and while they were eating, Sean told Ken that the "cave people" had hoped for rescue from the earth by some beings they called the Dods. Ken thought that was very strange. They were now all cooling their heels in the local jail. Sean told Ken that he was going to visit them. Ken admired Sean for wanting to continue to speak with his former captors. Ken was even more surprised when Sean said that he'd not bring any charges against them for kidnapping him. Ken was so in awe of this man. He didn't know what to say to him.

After their lunch, Ken informed Sean that he had decided that he would leave his little home and move on to another place. He was restless for a new adventure. Sean was surprised by this sudden decision and he inquired as to where Ken would live. Ken said that he would either go to Egypt or Greece. He wasn't sure but he knew that he'd seen enough of Switzerland and he wanted to explore an entirely new culture in another country. He told Sean that he'd definitely keep in touch with him. Sean told Ken that he'd like to keep in contact with him.

Ken was able to sell his home and within a month he was on his way to Egypt. He had made arrangements to rent an apartment in Cairo. He had the travelling bug and he wanted to explore, explore and never to meet strange people again. However, as was always the case, Ken knew in his heart that he was sure to be disappointed on that score!

Chapter Thirty-Six
Heat!

As Ken stepped from the plane at the Cairo airport, a warm wind struck him and almost caught him off guard. It was sure different from Switzerland. There was a lot of noise and hustle and bustle as he tried to catch a cab to his apartment. Finally he got one and he was on his way. The driver spoke some broken English and he was able to tell him that there was a sand storm in the desert and that was why it was so windy. Ken didn't like the idea of sand storms. When he got to his apartment he was able to get into it right away without too much trouble. The landlord was helpful and he pointed out the attributes of the apartment. It was furnished and as it was on the top floor, it had a roof top deck from which the whole city could be viewed as well as out into the desert areas. He didn't really notice that the apartment was "frayed around the edges" and that if he stood still and listened, he could hear many sounds from both inside and outside the building. All he wanted to do was to clean up and explore his new surroundings. He had not brought much with him as he had learned to travel light.

After a refreshing shower, Ken went into the street to find a place to eat as he was very hungry. He found a small cafe on a nearby corner. The food was delicious and the people were friendly. He would have to get used to the constant hum of activity that seemed to be everywhere. The smells he encountered overwhelmed his nostrils. A mixture of jasmine, tobacco, spices and the polluted air of this city of sixteen million was overwhelming to one who had so recently been in the clean, crisp air of Switzerland. Ken wandered out into the nearby streets looking at the various items vendors were hawking. He bought a colorful piece of material (after a lot of bargaining) to put up over his windows as a curtain of sorts. After his stroll about the city streets, he found himself to be extremely fatigued, dripping in sweat and so he went back to his apartment and fell into his bed and into dreamland.

He woke up late the next morning and he found that it was already hot and humid. He had a shower and then he threw open his windows but that didn't do much good. He would have to invest in some air conditioning equipment. This wasn't the best apartment he could have rented and he wondered if he should hunt for a better one. His landlord greeted him profusely on the stairs as he went down to find some late breakfast. Ken inquired as to what was used for air conditioning. The landlord laughed as he told him that such items were hard to get but he could buy fans. Ken wondered how much good fans would help the situation. He had noticed air conditioning units on the buildings in the area.

As Ken was eating his breakfast he thought that he'd just rent out a hotel suite for a month to see if he liked it there and if he wanted to stay longer in Egypt he'd look for a house. He quickly arranged to go to a big hotel near the Nile River. He paid off his landlord and took a cab to the hotel. The cab driver was very skillful in weaving in and out of the thick traffic. He used his horn a lot. He told Ken that there was a law about not using horns but no one really adhered to it. Ken was thankful that he arrived safely at the hotel. He was looking forward to more comfortable surroundings.

Happily, Ken was able to come to an agreement with the hotel for a good rate for a month's stay. He was able to get a top floor suite. It was wonderfully cool, clean and tastefully furnished. Ken noticed how quiet it was and that it had its own kitchen. There was a laundry service, too. Ken was pleased. He decided to get some information from the front desk about tourist spots and activities. The hotel ran tours and so he got some brochures and then he headed for one of the hotel's many restaurants. He was very hungry. He always enjoyed experiencing new foods from different countries and here he could sample food from a buffet. He enjoyed his meal immensely. He could have eaten another of the nut pastries. The cafe wasn't crowded that day and so he chatted with the waiter and he found out that he also was a tour guide. He told Ken that he was going to lead a group that would explore the main attractions of Cairo. The tour would start in two hours.

Ken set off on the tour with a chatty group from all over the world. He got to sit right at the front of the tour van and watch how the driver managed to swerve and dodge traffic, people and animals. The tour guide rattled on about the sights as they passed them. They stopped at the Egyptian Museum. Ken was eager to see all the sights from ancient Egypt. After a half hour of examining all the artifacts Ken was amazed by all the industry these ancient people had put into their representations of their beliefs. Only the best materials and the most ambitious endeavours had produced these astonishing remnants of a time long ago. Although he knew Egyptian history quite well, he was almost dumbstruck by the fact that he was actually looking at its history. If these statues could speak what would they say and what would they warn everyone about what not to do and what should be done in this life to prepare for the next life? These were the musings running in Ken's mind. After all, their history was all about the next life. Where were they now? He ran over these questions in his mind all that afternoon.

They visited several other museums and by supper time Ken and his tour companions were exhausted. The heat combined with the pollution haze was oppressive. Thankfully, the tour guide led them to an air conditioned restaurant where they all enjoyed a light supper and cool drinks. Ken enjoyed chatting with everyone and he got to be friendly with several of them who wanted to go on some adventures with him in the Cairo area. As he was talking to a young couple from the United States he caught sight of two people out of the corner of his eye. They looked faintly recognizable somehow. They were very large and jolly. Their laughs were heard by everyone in the restaurant. Suddenly, a cold shiver went through Ken. It all came back to him. He knew these two men! He searched his mind for connections and then … he remembered! They must be Brother Happy and Brother Mirth!! They had been members of the Yellow Group. Those days seemed so far away and yet everything came back to Ken's remembrance and he relived the time he had spent so unhappily with the group devoted to the pursuit of joy. Ken felt physically ill. He excused himself and hailed a cab back to his hotel. What was he going to do? It wasn't the heat of this city that was getting to him but rather the heat he felt as he contemplated the horrible thought that he had almost been recognized by these two kooks!

Chapter Thirty-Seven
Escape Into the Desert?

The horror of realizing that those two loons were in the same city as he was sent Ken into a mild depression. All he could do was to try and not meet up with them. What were they doing here? They appeared to be by themselves. Were they trying to recruit new members to their crazy cult? Maybe they wanted to climb one or all of the pyramids? Ken pushed that thought out of his head. There certainly must be laws about not entering into such "activities". He lay in his bed and stared at the ceiling. Maybe he should just take a cruise down the Nile. After mulling that over for a while he decided that he'd do just that and he went downstairs to the lobby to make arrangements.

Ken froze in his tracks as he saw them at the main counter! He hid behind a huge potted palm and tried to hear what they were talking about with the desk clerk. He hear the words, "cruise" and "Nile" and a lot of laughing and giggling. Ken had heard enough. He definitely was not going on a cruise and he wasn't going to stay at this hotel any longer. Obviously they were guests there, too. Then suddenly, Ken almost shook himself and he found himself thinking that these two were controlling him. He'd stay right where he was and do what he liked and they would not dictate his decisions. However, he was going to stay as far away from them as was possible.

Ken slipped by them and headed towards the tourist counter, all the while hoping that they would not see him. He was reading about tours down the Nile and guided tours of the pyramids when he saw that the two loons were almost beside him! He turned away and edged towards the end of the counter. They were guffawing over one of the pictures in a pamphlet. Apparently the picture of a pyramid had caused them to go into gales of laughter. People were turning their heads and staring at them. The two men were unaware of any stares.

They were punching the air and slapping each other on their backs. Ken stared at them from over a pamphlet and then he started to tremble. Several other people had joined the jolly men and they were all whooping and hollering, too. Ken faintly remembered some of these people from the Yellow Group! Was that Brother Joyous? Where those two women Sister Laughter and Sister Merry Merry? But what really caught Ken's attention was that there seemed to be some others there from the days of the pyramid group. Were these joined groups? There were about forty people standing around by the time everyone got together. Due to the commotion that they had caused, they were ushered out of the lobby area by several porters. Ken wondered if other groups had joined the Yellow Group. What was going on? Was this a "convention" of some kind? Ken was oddly curious, although he knew better that to get even remotely mixed up in finding out what they had planned for themselves in Egypt! Then Ken had a wild idea. Perhaps they were all going to try to ascend the tallest pyramid in Egypt! Of course it was impossible but they could be deluded enough to try such a fool-hardy escapade!

Ken decided that a trip to the pyramids was in order. Maybe if he saw the groups he could warn the officials. He knew that was a stretch but he set about his plans and by the next day he was in van with a small group headed toward "pyramid country"; the Giza Plateau. Of course it was hot and dusty but Ken was excited. He saw travelling groups of camels and off in the distance he saw the pyramids stretching into the sky. They rose from the desert like blurred triangles in the shimmering heat. Ken couldn't believe that he was actually on his way to see a real pyramid! He snapped as many pictures as he could and as were allowed. Finally they had arrived at their first pyramid. Their guide gathered the group together to spell out the rules of the pyramid tours. There were a lot of them! He fleetingly thought about how the kooks were going to try something sneaky with all these "guidelines".

Ken's group headed towards the nearest pyramid. They were allowed to enter by one entrance only and they were not to go ahead of the guide. It was the Great Pyramid of Khufu. They entered the Grand Gallery and at the top of it they entered a low hallway of sorts which led into the King's Chamber. The walls were made of polished granite. Ken peered into the large sarcophagus. It was made of granite also and the guide informed them that no burial items had ever been found. Ken guessed that robbers had found them first! After the tour, the group emerged blinking into the hot desert air and the sun beat down on them without mercy. Beggars and merchants nagged at tourists to part with their money. Ken felt irritated by the constant bother of trying to evade their pleas.

As Ken was examining a large cedar boat, just outside the pyramid and which had been the King's possession, a crowd of noisy tourists were heard before they were seen. They were supposed to be lined up for entrance into the pyramid but they were all bunched together at the front of the lineup. They were being redirected to line up at the end of the line but they weren't listening to anyone but themselves. To Ken's horror he saw that they were all wearing different colored tee shirts. These colors were familiar to Ken and then he knew in his inner being that The Groups had come together for a special reason. There only seemed to be about twelve people. Maybe they had been specially selected for this "adventure".

Finally The Groups were brought under control but they were still grumbling at the back of the line. The tour was able to get under way. Ken wondered what would happen in there and if they had planned something to occur then or later or whenever they could "arrange" it. Ken wanted to make sure that The Groups emerged from the pyramid and so left his group after the tour was finished. He wasn't going to see the other two large pyramids: the pyramids of Khafre and Menkaure. He would miss out seeing the Sphinx as well but he wanted to observe what was going on and his group had to go on without him. After a while, the last members of the tour emerged from the exit doorway. Ken did not see one colored shirt! Some officials were heard yelling inside the pyramid. Apparently, The Groups had lingered too long and they were now being escorted out by several soldiers. There was a lot of grumbling and some resistance was going on but all of them finally, gradually, emerged and Ken breathed a sigh of relief.

Ken thought that an escapade in a real pyramid would be exactly what The Groups wanted as after all, the ancient Kings were thought to use them as a sort of stairway to the stars. Surely a trip as tourists wasn't their goal. Ken decided to stay in a hotel near the pyramids to observe what would or would not occur. He ate his supper at a restaurant that overlooked the pyramids. There was a light show that night and the pyramids looked eerie as they were bathed in various colors. Ken wondered what the ancient Egyptians would think about all this strange activity. Ken went to his room and thought about what he would do the next day.

Ken ran into The Groups the next day as they were hanging around his hotel. He could hear them talking about going south but then others wanted to stay and go out into the desert on camels. Ken observed the entire group listening to Brother Joyous talking about the merits of staying put and planning their next "adventure" as he put it. They all broke out into cheers when he mentioned an "adventure". Ken was worried. He was going to keep a sharp eye on them.

Later that evening Ken observed the "selected ones" (probably the twelve chosen ones) from the Group of Groups heading toward the three smaller pyramids on the eastern side of the pyramid of Khufu. Ken remembered that the guide said that these three pyramids were probably constructed for three queens. What were they up to? Ken waited for their return but they did not return to the hotel that evening. Ken decided that he'd investigate. He would try to find out where they were and what they were doing around these ancient monuments. Surely they wouldn't be able to stay around the pyramids for long.

When it got dark Ken crept out into the area of the pyramids. He had brought a small flashlight with him and a water bottle. As he got nearer to the most northerly pyramid, he noticed that there were no tourists anywhere. This pyramid might have belonged to Khufu's mother. He also noticed that there were guards at all the entrances. Lights lit up the area and so it was difficult to creep around unnoticed. He managed to hide at the corner of the pyramid. He saw nothing out of order. It was about midnight when he felt safe enough to venture out of his hiding place. There were three guards standing together talking and smoking. Ken had time to try and find an entrance. He saw a way of access in the north wall. Carefully, he flattened his body against the wall and slipped inside the "entrance". It was totally pitch black and so he used his flashlight. He waved it around as he descended into what seemed a path that led down and then he found himself turning toward the right. He thought that he heard some rustling sounds but he ignored them. He was having a hard time breathing and he knew he'd have to get out of there as soon as possible. He had come into an area that might have been a burial chamber. Ken almost jumped when he heard a muffled giggle! Ken felt himself tense up and he started to sweat even more than he already was and he trembled to think that he was caught in this confining space with THEM! He decided to get out of there as quickly as possible. He thought that these people were in danger of suffocating. It would be a tight fit. He managed to climb up the dry and dusty passageway and finally he reached the "entrance". Suddenly, hands gripped him around his neck! One of them had probably followed him. He struggled with every nerve and muscle and he managed somehow to get outside.

Ken knew what he had to do as he had gone through this "drill" many times before when dealing with these "cults". He ran as fast as his trembling legs could go towards the guards and yelled at them to get their attention. They were astonished to see him and they ran towards him with their guns leveled at him. Fortunately, one of them could speak English.

Chapter Thirty-Eight
Turmoil

Ken was able to make the guards understand what was going on in the pyramid. Reinforcements were marshaled and the pyramid was surrounded. An ultimatum was shouted out over a megaphone. The Groups were told to surrender immediately or a forced entrance would occur in order to remove them. The "army" waited and waited. Not a sound was heard. Finally, two people emerged and they looked like they were about to faint. They sat down in front of the pyramid and couldn't or wouldn't move. Over the next few minutes the rest of invaders struggled out of the pyramid. They all seemed to be out but Ken knew that there must be at least four more of them in the pyramid. After everyone was given water and something to eat they were taken away in vans to the nearest police station. Ken tried to make the officials understand that there were more of the invaders inside of the pyramid. Finally, they believed him and several of them entered into the pyramid. They emerged with two men. Ken felt sure that Brother Joyous and possibly one or two others were either in the pyramid or they had somehow escaped. He couldn't make the officials go in for another look as everyone was exhausted and the sun was now up and a new day had arrived.

 Ken decided to go to the police station and see if he could spot who was missing from the "adventurers". He was able to view all of them from an observation room and he could not find Brother Joyous. Ken thought that he most probably had escaped. He wondered how the robust members, like Brother Joyous (who had gained weight) had even managed to maneuver in the pyramid. The captured were making a lot on noise and causing confusion by singing a strange song out of tune. The song got louder and louder until finally they were silenced by an officer shouting at them through a large megaphone. Then they were ordered into a cell where they were to experience great discomfort. They were all together in a large cell. They all sat down on the floor of their cell and moaned and wailed piteously. Ken knew it was all a planned protest. Ken had to get out of that place and so he headed back to his hotel. He had kept as far away as possible from them at all times so that they would, hopefully, never recognize him.

As Ken ate a late breakfast he wondered what he would do next. There was no way he'd go back to that pyramid. He had told an English-speaking official at the police station about his suspicions about the Yellow Group leaders. They would have to investigate. Ken knew it was time to move on and to get away from this whole area. He headed back to Cairo and went to his room. He tried to catch up on his lost sleep but he found himself having nightmares about strange songs and hands grabbing at him in the dark. He woke up with a start when he heard a commotion outside of his room.

Ken carefully walked toward his door and peered out the eyehole to view the hallway. To his astonishment he saw Brother Joyous and two men from his group having an argument right near his door! He was looking at wanted men and they were right there! They were yelling about the prisoners and escaping and the police. Ken surmised that they were deciding what they should do about their fellow "adventurers". Ken tiptoed to his phone and alerted the front desk. He was told to lie on the floor far way from the door. He waited a few minutes and then he heard commands being shouted and then running steps away down the hall and then there was silence.

Ken phoned the desk and found out that the men had been chased out of the building and that was all they knew about what had happened. They assured Ken that the hotel was quite safe as there was a lot of security around and in it. Ken pondered about what to do next. He had had enough of this upheaval. He began thinking about moving on and leaving Egypt. He had enjoyed the sights and sounds and the experience of looking at historical landmarks but now he was not as keen to explore any more places in Egypt as he might come across THEM. No doubt the "adventurers" would be freed and perhaps deported and they would be let loose on the world again. When would he find a place on this Earth where there was a "no-groups" zone? His head ached and he felt that he was in a state of internal turmoil all the time. He was getting jumpy and nervous.

Chapter Thirty-Nine
A Change

The next day, at breakfast, Ken was reading an English newspaper and his eye caught an advertisement for art instructors in Israel. He had never thought about going to Israel but as he read about the job he thought that it sounded great. They would provide everything he needed and they needed someone as soon as possible. It was a Government job. Ken decided to apply that day. For the rest of the day Ken did some artwork in his room. He used some of the pictures that he had taken as his inspiration. He was pleased with the results. He hadn't painted in a long time and it was great to be involved in a relaxing pursuit and he forgot about his recent difficulties as he sketched and painted. Before he knew it, the day was almost done and he hadn't even noticed the passage of time.

He had been in contact with Sean and Sean encouraged him to go to Israel. Sean told him that soon he'd be taking some of the people from his church on a tour of Jerusalem and its surroundings. The next day Ken learned that he'd be having a telephone interview about the job and he was excited. He mentally prepared himself to answer the questions he thought they'd ask him. He was ready when the phone call came through and he thought that he had done well when it was finished. Now he only had to wait and see if he'd be going to Israel. He spent the day picking up a few souvenirs and taking more pictures.

After Ken had enjoyed a great supper, he went to his room and he found out that there was a telephone message for him. He contacted the number but there was no answer as it was after office hours. It was the office he had been talking to in Israel. That night seemed to drag on forever but finally after hours of tossing and turning in his bed, Ken woke from his ragged sleep to see the sun blazing into his windows and as he looked at his clock he noticed that it was already nine o'clock! He jumped into his clothes and decided to call the number.

After a few minutes he was talking to the Dean of students who invited him to come to Jerusalem to teach art! Ken was overjoyed! He thanked the man and told him he'd be there the next day if possible.

Ken's mind raced. He quickly got his travel plans arranged, ate a very late breakfast, packed and hailed a cab to the airport. He was on his way to new experiences in a land he had never thought he'd ever see! It was very hot and muggy as he neared the airport but Ken didn't mind. He was walking in a haze of his own. He waited in the waiting room for his plane and he could hardly keep his feet from tapping in his nervousness. He was off to The Holy Land!

Finally, Ken was able to relax when he got onto the airplane. He was given a window seat. As the plane taxied down the runway, Ken felt that this was the right plan. He was going to do something that he'd never done before and he was looking forward to the changes that would come into his life. It was late in the afternoon when Ken got onto his plane and as the plane lifted off the runway, Egypt passed below him in a blur of brown and green and Ken smiled to himself. This job in Israel might turn out to be his greatest adventure!

Chapter Forty
Adjustments

Ken arrived very late that day and so he arranged to stay in a hotel for one night before going to his school. He was so tired that he fell asleep as soon as his head hit the pillow. He hadn't really taken in the sights as it was dark when he had arrived in Israel. It was all a blur. However, when the sun streamed through his window Ken was awake and ready for this new day. He was in West Jerusalem. He contacted his school and said that he'd be there within a few hours.

After eating his breakfast Ken got his luggage together and headed for the lobby to wait for the cab he had ordered. He hoped that he could communicate with the driver. He was fortunate to get a driver who had immigrated from the U.S. and no language problem existed. As they made their way through the busy streets, Ken and his driver conversed about all the sights he could see while he was in the country. The driver, David, told him that there were different districts in Jerusalem. There was the Old City, West Jerusalem or New Jerusalem, East Jerusalem, home to many Arabs, the Me'a Shearim area populated by ultra-Orthodox Jews, The German Colony in West Jerusalem and Ein Kerem in West Jerusalem which was the home of many artistic people. Ken was headed towards that area. He was getting excited.

Ken was pleasantly surprised by the modern buildings and lush setting of his new home. He walked into the foyer of the college and rang the bell. An older woman with a huge smile welcomed him and led him to an inner office. He waited just outside of it and wondered who he was going to meet next in this college. A middle-aged bearded man came out of the inner office door and gave Ken a firm handshake and ushered him into the inner office. The man introduced himself as David Bergman. He was the Dean of the Art Department. He told Ken that they were excited to have him as a Visiting Artist. He would have twenty students in an advanced art class to teach and to guide. Ken was very pleased when he heard that there were separate apartments for the Staff on the campus. He could cook his own food or take his meals in the college's cafeteria. His pay was going to be quite generous. Students came from around the world to study at this college.

After the meeting Ken went to see his apartment and he was pleasantly surprised by the coziness of it and the spaciousness it afforded him to paint and to prepare for his classes. It was tastefully furnished and had everything he needed. He sat down at his kitchen table and wondered to himself about the "miracle" that had brought him to live here in the Holy Land. Ken nearly pinched himself to see if this was all real. Most of his own cooking could be done and so he had to get some food. He headed toward the main foyer and there he inquired as to where he could shop for food and he was directed to the nearest local market. An outdoor market was just two streets away and there, he was told, he would find everything he needed to prepare his meals.

When he got there he was surprised by the variety of foods displayed in the open stalls. He gaped at the fish heads and hanging chicken carcasses. Every fruit and vegetable grown in Israel seemed to be there and he got to sample some of them. He matched prices and was able to get some deals. He had three bulging bags of food by the time he was finished. There was a lot of noise and banter and everyone was in a great mood. Ken was eager to get back to his new apartment and begin cooking.

When he arrived back at his apartment there was a telephone message for him and he found out that he was invited to supper at the Dean's house. Ken put away his food purchases and got ready for his first social contact with the staff of the college. He showered and changed into a bright colored shirt and tan slacks and headed out for the Dean's house which was only a block away from the campus. He arrived right on time and gave the hostess some fruit he had purchased at the market. There were twelve people there and introductions began as soon as he entered the area at the back of the house where everyone was gathered. Ken was not good at remembering names but he didn't forget faces. Some of the staff members were from other countries. All of the staff spoke in English much to Ken's relief. Everyone was very friendly and they gave him tips about life in Jerusalem. Soon they were all laughing together as if they had known each other since childhood. The meal was so delicious that Ken asked for some recipes. Several of the staff members joked that they'd be at his apartment for meals when they learned that he liked to do his own cooking. It was quite late when Ken and several of the staff members left together to go to their apartments. They learned that they all lived close to one another. Ken was happy about his first day in Jerusalem. There were nice people around him, he was getting to teach young people about art and he was sure that he was going to enjoy every minute of his time in this enchanted place.

Chapter Forty-One
Eager Minds

Ken spent the next day preparing some lessons for his first classes which would commence the following day. He invited two of the young teachers to supper. They were both Americans from the mid West and they too were going to be teaching at the college for the first time. The three of them decided that when they had time off they would go exploring together. There would be so much to see and experience and they all wanted to do as much as was possible during their time there. Ken was so wound up by the end of the evening that he couldn't go to sleep. He stared at the ceiling for a long time. Tomorrow would be a day like never before in his life. This was a new chapter full of promise and fulfillment. He would be helping young people to grow in their artistic skills. He felt like the former misadventures and traumas of his life were ended and that he could now create positive memories. Surely here he would not be hounded by pests from the past.

The next day Ken met his first class and he was pleasantly surprised to see that they were all from North America. He could relate to them about certain geographical and cultural areas and they of course, all spoke English. Ken presented his introductory lecture and he was encouraged by the prospect of teaching these eager students. He went to the cafeteria with several of them and they had a great time laughing together. Ken promised to bring some of his recent paintings to the next class. The rest of his art and possessions were in storage in Switzerland. As he was talking to the students Ken thought of taking pictures of the places he would explore and then do a series of paintings for a possible book. During the afternoon he conducted two other classes and he was just as impressed with the students who were from all over the world. After his classes he went to his little office to be available to students and to do some more preparation for future classes.

Tom Whitehead, a professor who had recently arrived from England, popped into Ken's office and invited him to "tea" with his family. Ken accepted the invitation gladly and he spent a wonderful time with Tom's and Judy's energetic children who were all under the age of nine years. They went to a school nearby and seemed to be getting along well with their classmates and adjusting to the school system. As he sipped tea and munched on sausages and chips he imagined himself having such a family. His thoughts inadvertently drifted to Star and he decided to call her to find out how she was coping with life. He had not contacted her for a quite a while.

That night Ken called Star and found that her phone number had been disconnected and he wondered where she might have gone and how he was going to find out about her whereabouts. She had never given Ken an email address, which Ken had always felt was strange. Something must be wrong. Ken was worried but he was helpless to do anything about it. He mused to himself about these things as he prepared for the next day.

The students began showing Ken their artistic talents and Ken was impressed. Their assignments were always done well and they put great effort into each one of them. Not one of them seemed to be there just for "the ride". Ken decided to challenge them by giving them more demanding assignments. He planned to go on a field trip with them to one of the many ancient sites in this special land. He got permission to go to Petra with two of his classes and two other professors would be going along as well. Two buses were hired and preparations were made for the big adventure. Ken spent the next two days finalizing paperwork, making calls and getting permission for the students to paint on the site. He was tired before the adventure had even started but he was looking forward to seeing these ancient ruins in Jordan.

The day of the big adventure dawned and Ken was up at the crack of dawn. He met the students and the professors at the two parked buses in front of the college. They were all a very sleepy crew. Many of the students had managed to grab large coffees to keep themselves awake. There was a low buzz of chatter as Ken told everyone to get onto their assigned buses. He gave the occupants of each bus the same instructions as to when they would arrive and he handed out schedules which indicated where and when they would be that day. They would be away for several days on their great adventure. Everyone cheered as the buses headed out of the college driveway and headed towards the nearest highway. Ken sat at the front of the first bus and chatted with the driver and the students around him. After a while many of the passengers got quiet and caught up on some much needed sleep. They probably were dreaming of the rose-red city carved from rocks.

Chapter Forty-Two
Astonishing Revelations

As they headed East Ken mused about why the ancients would try so hard to cut or carve edifices out of rock. Then his mind drifted toward some of the caves he had encountered during the past several years. He thought about the people who had decided to live in them and he wondered if there was a connection as to why people wanted to get away into areas that were in high places or led to higher places. Perhaps he would learn something on this trip. Perhaps he would connect the pieces of the puzzle that was always in the back of his mind. Why did people do these strange things? What were they searching for and why did they try so hard to find it? There were over eight hundred monuments at Petra. All of them were carved out sandstone. Ken would see the evidence of Assyrian, Egyptian, Hellenistic and Roman cultures there and he knew that they would all have left their particular "marks" on the site. Sean had told him an interesting fact about Petra. It used to be a part of Seir or Edom. Descendants of Esau lived in Edom. Edom stretched from the south of Judah to the Dead Sea and then to the Gulf of Aqaba. Ken made a mental note to find out more about Esau.

Before they all knew it they were in Eliat and crossing over to Aqaba, Jordan. After paperwork had been processed (which seemed to take forever) the group ate their packed lunches in the shade of their buses. It was very hot and the sun seemed to be penetrating their clothes right through to their bodies. They drank a lot of water. Then it was time to travel to Petra on the Desert Highway. The buses were climbing steadily and some of the students didn't want to look down into the valleys below the highway. Some overturned cars were seen beside the highway at several points. Speeders were caught by waiting police cars which were in hidden locations along the highway. As they neared Petra the excitement rose in the buses. Cameras were already snapping pictures of the surrounding countryside. There were loud cries when some Bedouin cowboys were seen riding their horses. They were riding fast and they looked like super heroes chasing some invisible villain. The buses made their way to the Visitors' Centre. They were at Petra!

Everyone lined up to pay the entrance fee and then they were on their way! The first part of the tour was through the gap made famous by the towering rock faces above them. They all felt like little ants as they peered up at the rock formations above and all around them. All seemed very hushed as if they were entering a time zone from somewhere else in space and it was as if they were all transported back into other times. They felt like they were being watched by unseen eyes. Through the 1200 meter long narrow gorge (or gap) called The Siq the group made their way in wonderment. They looked up to the eighty meter cliffs complete with carvings and water channels. After craning their necks to see the different geological formations and colorations of the sandstone rocks, the group gradually saw some light coming from the end of the Siq. As they got closer a feeling of something unusual came upon them and as they got nearer they could see the pale rose color of parts of the Treasury or the Al-Khazneh (Pharaoh's Treasury) emerge into their view. And suddenly there is was in all its eerie glory. It had been built as a royal tomb sometime between 100 BC and 200 AD. It was called the Treasury because it was thought that bandits had hidden their stolen booty in the stone urn (now very damaged due to gunshots aimed at it over the years) on the second level. The dimensions of this "doorway" were about 30 m wide and about 43 m high. The tomb was carved for a Nabataean King. Ken tried to imagine all the labour involved in carving it out of the rock. The students drew quick sketches and took pictures. Then it was time to see more sights.

Beside the Outer Siq they came to a place called the Street of Faces or Street of Facades which consisted of four rows, one row over the other along the face of the cliff. They were Nabataean tombs with a lot of detailed carvings. They all gaped at the outdoor theatre carved into the solid rock. It could have been built by the Romans. It was quite large and it would have held many people. As Ken was looking at the outdoor theatre and wondering what went on in this place he heard his name being called and he turned in the direction of the voice and then he saw to his astonishment that it was Sean! Sean ran toward him and hugged him and laughed loudly at Ken's surprise. Sean had his little group in tow and introductions were made as Ken and some of the students exchanged hellos with the group from Switzerland. Ken's group had seen many sights and they were on their way back to their hotel. Ken realized that the hotel he would be spending several nights at was quite close to Sean's hotel. They arranged to meet the next evening for supper at one of the restaurants.

The next day Ken led his group on to see the many other attractions of this ancient and mysterious place. Because the Petra basin held over 800 monuments, Ken had to keep his group moving ahead! They wouldn't be able to see everything in one day! They saw more tombs. In fact there were five hundred tombs in Petra. The Urn Tomb had remained intact because it was built so high and therefore tomb robbers had had difficulty getting to it. The group was getting tired and the sun was beating down on them and so Ken called a quick meeting to assess what the group wanted to do next. All agreed that they should go back to the town and settle into their hotel and come back the next day to complete their tour. Ken agreed that it was worth paying the fees again as they all wanted to have detailed memories and sketches and perhaps the beginnings on some paintings before leaving this Wonder of the World. The other professors agreed and they and Ken led their groups away towards the gap and to their buses.

Ken was glad when his group was all settled, fed and watered. Then he could have some time for himself. He lay down for a nap but he kept staring at the whirling fan in the ceiling and trying to put his mind back into the past and what it was like to live in this area and what the people feared and what they lived for and how long they had happy periods or if they ever did have peaceful lives. Somehow he felt sadness for this place as he thought that it must have been a hard existence filled with terror and cruelty. That was what he felt and he couldn't shake these intense "impressions" that filled his whole being. It seemed these astonishing revelations and feelings were almost more that he could bear. Sometimes he thought that he was too sensitive. Then he decided that he'd share his feelings with Sean. Sean always carefully listened to him and he was so wise.

Chapter Forty-Three
Harsh Realities

He met Sean that night in the hotel's restaurant and they had a wonderful time. He was looking forward to viewing the rest of Petra's sites the next day. He wanted to talk to Sean alone and so he invited him to his room for a chat. Sean listened carefully as Ken told him about his intense feelings he had about Petra. Sean told him that he felt the same feelings and that he knew that the people had had hard lives and probably lived in fear. Then Sean told Ken something that caused him to sit up and listen intensely. The people of those days, Sean said, were just like people of all times and places and even like the people of this present time. They feared the unknown, death and they wanted to insure their safety in this life and in the life to come by performing rituals to appease whatever powers they thought controlled them. He told Ken that when he got to the place of sacrifice tomorrow, he'd understand, perhaps, what went on there so long ago. He hinted that there was an answer to the questions of life and death but that he'd talk to Ken about that after he had finished his tour of Petra. Sean's group would be there for two more days and so Ken would be able to compare "notes" with Sean after tomorrow's excursion. Ken felt somewhat better after his talk with Sean but his mind kept whirling as he tried to get some much needed sleep.
    The next day the group was eager to complete their tour of the sites of Petra. From the theater they climbed up and up to the High Place of Sacrifice. It took them about half an hour to get to the summit of the Attuf Ridge. The mountain scenery was splendid to view as they neared the summit. They had traveled along paths and stairways along the original Nabataean pathway that was used for processions. The first two monuments that caught their eyes were the two seven meter high rock obelisks. They had been carved out of the surface of the mountain which left two towering rocks. Across a gully was the High

Place of Sacrifice. Some said that it might have dated back to the time of the Edomites. The rock was leveled to form a courtyard-like setting with benches which faced the altar platform. Animal sacrifices were made on the platform. They were sacrificed (slaughtered) for the gods. There was a cistern near the platform that had provided water which was used in their ritual ceremony. Ken mused about the sacrifice of life on a high place to appease unknown powers which these people worshipped and feared at the same time. He'd have to ask Sean about all of this as he couldn't wrap his head around all of this religious worship. Ken was interrupted in his troubled musings by the lick of a donkey on his arm! He guessed it was waiting for a treat - maybe an apple. Ken was sorry that he didn't have anything to offer it. The donkey looked at him for a moment and then trotted off to find other tourists who might feed him. Ken could see the Royal Tombs from where he stood and he wanted to explore them. He rounded up his students who were making quick sketches and marveling at all that was around them.

On the way to the Royal Tombs they climbed up to the Al-Deir or The Monastery. He found it very haunting and he tried to imagine what might have gone on there so long ago. Even though it was a Nabataean structure, it was used by Christians in the Byzantine era. It had been a fatiguing climb to get there but it was worth it to see the Al-Deir rising in front of him. It had been cut into the mountainside. He felt so small looking up at it. This temple or perhaps, a tomb, was undecorated but arresting in its presentation. It seemed so massive and the door was said to be over eight meters high. Ken could envision processions of pilgrims coming up to the area in front of it and a feeling of awe overcoming them. He could see for miles around and he was awestruck by the loneliness and the beauty of this place. After they left that area Ken mused about the effort that those of long ago had put into carving out and creating these structures. It always seemed that almost super human efforts had to be made to create these high places of worship and sacrifice. He still did not know the answer as to the "why" of it all. Or perhaps he didn't want to believe what Sean had said as he thought it was too simplistic.

The rest of the day passed by and Ken felt very hungry and exhausted. He met with Sean and told him about his feelings. Sean nodded knowingly as if he knew about Ken's internal struggle. Ken still couldn't comprehend the "force" that drove peoples from all times and places to erect monuments to unknown gods. People went on pilgrimages to high places, sacrificed at high places and stood in high places to commune with the unknown and struggled to build communities and ways of life in high places. Ken felt that if he could understand this phenomenon, then he would understand a great mystery and he would be enlightened in some manner. It possibly could change his life. His life seemed to have been leading up to this understanding and he felt resolution might be near. It seemed just beyond his grasp. It felt like a fog that he wanted to walk right through and into sunlight and wisdom.

Sean told him about other cultures such as the Incas and the Hindus who trekked high into high places. Ken realized that he could spend the rest of his life visiting these places. But Sean brought him back to the history of the first peoples of the very land that they were visiting. The Israelites were told to conquer the land because its peoples were idolatrous. What did these ancient peoples do that was so evil that God declared that conquering some of them was the only solution? It very much involved "worship" which sometimes included human sacrifice in high places to false gods. Ken felt that now he was finally coming to an understanding and his troubled mind and heart would be at rest and he would find the peace he had so longed for all of his life. Sean kept on talking and Ken reaffirmed to himself that there definitely was a pattern in man's search for meaning. Sean said that God dwells in the highest of places and rules over all that He created. He created the sun and stars and He alone was to be worshipped. Ken realized the futility of the endeavours of all that he had witnessed in the erection of monuments, buildings, performance of rituals and belief systems that were based on the imagination of man's minds. As he was beginning to achieve some kind of understanding of man's search for meaning, Ken began to wonder what the answer was to the meaning of life on Earth and what would happen after one left it.

Sean and Ken parted company and the students and Ken returned to Jerusalem the next day. They were all exhausted but felt that they had learned so much. Ken was very quiet on the bus as he mused about what he had seen and had discussed with Sean. He was becoming restless again and wanted to have a change of scenery. He wondered where he would go next.

Chapter Forty-Four
A New Vision

As Ken taught his classes and interacted with his students and the staff, his mind was far off. He caught himself drifting in his thoughts right in the middle of teaching. The students had to get his attention to bring him back to reality. Ken had been thinking of another place to visit. Quite by accident or coincidence he had come across it in a book he had just been flipping through in the library. It was Megiddo. It was a place of enormous historical importance. As he read about it a longing to explore it filled him and he felt a pull towards that ancient place. The college break was coming soon. Fortunately, he was able to make travel arrangements without too many problems. In order to take in the full atmosphere of this unusual place, he'd go alone. The prospect of exploring this particular area excited him. There had been so many conflicts there and some said that the final conflict would happen in that very place. It had been a place of refuge and great loss. A week later he was heading toward the tour bus that would take him to this intriguing mount and plain.

Ken slept a lot during the two hour trip and only wakened at stops along the way. He was refreshed when the bus pulled into the National Park entrance. He jumped off the bus in eager anticipation. There was a tour guide who would lead them through the various sites. Ken had brought a lot of snacks and he had large water bottle. He was ready as he and his fellow travelers formed a line to go through the entrance. Ken was amazed at the view from the ruins. The valley below was laid out as if to invite a special event. Ken could imagine armies assembled there by the thousands. He felt like a fly on a rock as he peered down through the haze of the now-increasingly warm day. Ken had read thoroughly about the history of this place. He wanted to examine the remnants of the ancient Canaanite site which dated back to about 3,300 B.C. He especially wanted to explore the worship center. Ken could hardly get his head around the fact that there were twenty-five layers of settlements which had been built over thirty-five centuries. Overall, Megiddo or Har Megiddo (Mount Megiddo) could be dated back five thousand years!

As Ken drank a big gulp of water he looked up at the crumbling walls and wondered about those early city dwellers. He was tired from climbing and he rested against a wall and he tried to envisage what life was like when the city was being besieged. The tour was going on ahead of him and he was left by himself. He could catch up. As he gazed out across the wide expanse, he could see Mount Tabor and he knew that Nazareth was perched in the hills on his left. He knew that Megiddo was located right on the ancient Egypt-Syria highway. He could imagine the Egyptian chariots flying through the dust and into the Jezreel Valley and onto the plain of Esdraelon. Megiddo looked down on the Via Maris which was one of the major routes that was used for travel between Egypt, Syria and Mesopotamia. How the people must have cringed as yet another attack might be made upon their fortress! There was a record of the battle which resulted from the attack led by the Egyptian Pharaoh Thutmose III in 1479 B.C.E. Ken thought he could identify in some faint way with the feelings of dread and horror that surrounded this place. True, they had the advantage in many ways. They had a superb water system drawn from the Megiddo spring. Their walls were strong. They could see for miles. Ken was roused from his thoughts by shouts from members of his tour party. They wanted him to join them.

Ken joined the group at the place of ancient worship. It was a mysterious place, possibly used by the Canaanites. The "altar" was quite massive. What went on there? It was said to have been constructed in the Bronze Age about the third millennium B.C. The "altar" was ten meters in diameter. Ken went up the staircase and onto the platform of the "altar". This area was a religious complex used by priests so long ago. Ken's imagination could envisage solemn rituals being carried out especially if danger was nearby.

The most intriguing part of the tour was a seventy meter tunnel the group went through which was said to have been built by King Ahab in the ninth century, B.C. There were 183 steps into the shaft and then tunnel was another 215 feet. The shaft was 120 feet deep. It was part of the superb water system which was necessary to sustain the inhabitants especially if they were under attack. The people in the town would not have to leave the city walls to collect water. The engineering feats of these ancient peoples astounded Ken and the other members of the tour party. The engineers were able to find deep subterranean sources of water and to also tunnel to outside water sources. Ken was constantly amazed at the effort that early peoples put into their projects! They were very intelligent and creative as well as being pragmatic.

Ken was able to get near a recessed wall that was supposed to have been a part of the Solomonic Gate. He had gone through the inner and outer Solomonic Gates and had imagined long ago attackers passing through the outer area before trying to attack the inner main gate. There even was an area of Bronze Age gates, one of which could be dated back to the Middle or Late Bronze Ages. He visited the storerooms or possibly stables, at the north end of the complex. It was debatable as to whether they were Solomonic or from the time of Ahab. He was intrigued by the remains of what were most possibly, the posts where the horses were tied up and some troughs could be seen as well. There were also eastern storerooms or stables and Ken was very interested to find out that these eastern stables were said to have been built over the older Canaanite Temple complex. There were also southern storerooms or stables. Ken walked around a circular grain silo which was said to have existed from the days of Jeroboam. He walked down the Israelite staircase to what was said to have been a water collection area.

After all the walking Ken was hungry and very tired. The tour bus took the group back to their hotel and Ken caught up on his sleep. He decided to go back the next day to take more pictures and make some quick sketches. He was able to do this because the tour group had two flex days to do as they pleased before heading home. Ken was able to get some great pictures and he made numerous sketches the next day. He liked watching the shadows on the ancient stones and the gentle waving of palm trees. He looked up into the sky and something that Sean had quoted came to his memory. He thought for a moment and then he was able to put it together. It was from Amos four verse thirteen. Ken said these words to himself, "For, lo, he that formeth the mountains, and createth the wind, and declared unto man what is his thought, who maketh the morning darkness, and treadeth upon the high places of the earth, The LORD, The God of hosts, is his name." He had asked Sean what the part about declaring unto man about his thought meant and Sean had said that God knows all about us and everything we do and say and all about out past and our future. He had told Ken to read the hundred and thirty-ninth Psalm in the Bible. Ken hadn't done so but he vowed that he would when he got back to his hotel. He had been given a small Bible by Sean and although he hadn't read much in it until this point, he began to think that he should read it since he was in "the land of the Bible". Ken began to think that God was trying to get his attention somehow. If God was in control of everything past and present then he would have to explore getting to know Him or God would have to get his attention, perhaps even by "talking to him".

Chapter Forty-Five
New Views

Ken did read the hundred and thirty-ninth Psalm and found that its message was that he could never escape from the presence of God. He wasn't sure how he felt about that but it was comforting in some ways. Ken's mind was racing ahead to other places he wanted to visit. He wanted to visit Masada. He had run out of holidays and so he decided that his time at the school was over and at the end of the term he gave his notice in and said his goodbyes and he gathered up a few possessions and left for new adventures. He felt that he had to visit several other interesting high places to finally solve the meaning of all that he had seen and experienced in his life since he entered the Village of Wonder so long ago. Sometimes he thought that the whole Wonder chapter of his life had been a dream but Star was alive. After visiting these places he would make a decision and he knew it was going to be the decision of his life. Before going to Masada Ken was going to visit the Temple Mount. He knew it was a tourist magnet but he thought it would be helpful to go on a tour of all the significant sites in that area.

Ken's visit to the Temple Mount stirred him in many ways. He felt that this was a special place. Even the many tourists didn't bother him as he mused on the history of this ancient space of historical and spiritual significance. Sean had told him that in the future this would be a place of great significance even the culmination of all history. If the stones would only speak, what would they tell him? There was so much he didn't know and didn't understand. As he walked down through the narrow streets crowded with all manner of peoples he wondered what would happen to these streets and what had happened on them. He bought food from open stalls and wandered around trying to imprint this place's smells, noises and buildings upon his memory. He took a lot of pictures. He made short videos with his camera. He went to all the tourist sites and listened to the guides as they rattled on about the sacred history all around them. It didn't mean too much to him but he was somewhat amazed by the devotion and emotion of many of the tourists. Some were openly weeping. At the Wailing Wall he stopped and stared as the devoted prayed at it and he wondered what their prayers were about and why they thought that was the place to pray.

Ken went on a bus to his next destination which was Masada, an ancient defense position. As he headed toward south east toward the Dead Sea, Ken thought about the history of this place. Herod had developed this site to make it his royal citadel. It contained two palaces, towers, strong walls and aqueducts. The Romans took it over after Herod's death. In AD 66 the Zealots, a Jewish sect, took it over in a surprise attack. They refused to surrender to the Romans under Flavius Silva. It took two years to conquer the fortress. Ken tried to imagine how they survived there and how they were able to withstand the Romans for so long. How did they feel when the Romans built camps around the base of Masada and when they built a wall as well as a rampart that was set against the western side of the fortress? Ken imagined the horror of the spring of 74 AD when the Romans moved up the ramp with a battering ram and then roared over the wall of the fortress. The sad end of the thousand men, women and children who refused to be taken alive was truly horrific. They burned the fortress and their lives were lost. Eleazar ben Ya'ir had been their leader. The story of their deaths was one that had echoed down through the years. Ten men were chosen to kill the rest of the people. Then one was chosen from the ten to kill them and then that last Jew killed himself. Masada would always be a reminder of a people who wanted to be free in their own land.

After the bus arrived Ken jumped out of it and looked up at the fortress while his imagination kept running and he felt that he somehow could feel the fear of the people who knew that death was coming soon. He got onto the cable car that carried them up to the top of the rock and he looked out across the Dead Sea which was four hundred meters below sea level. He felt very alone as he surveyed the land and the magnificent view. He felt very high like an eagle, up above everything. When he got out of the cable car he paused to survey the area and he imagined the people long ago as they stood there and looked for the enemy. He remembered that he had read that the Arabs called the mountain: As-Sabba or "The Accursed". The story of this place probably would not have been told except for the survival of two women and five children who had all hidden in a water conduit. Ken eagerly joined the tour group as they headed up one of trails called the "Snake Path" on the North East side of the mesa. Ken was glad that the whole area had been excavated and there were many places to stop and look at what remains had been found and preserved. He took many pictures that day as he wanted to remember this day and never forget it. He was intrigued by the synagogue which was in the northwestern section of the casemate wall (which were two parallel walls with partitions which had rooms between them). The synagogue was situated so that it was turned toward Jerusalem. He was interested to learn that fragments of two scrolls which contained portions of Deuteronomy and Ezekiel 37 had been found hidden in pits that had been dug under the floor of a small room inside the synagogue. Ken told himself to look up that chapter in Ezekiel to find out what it contained. He was fascinated by the display of artifacts that had been found and which gave him an idea of how they lived and the utensils, tools and weapons that they had used. Due to the dry climate there had been many things that had been preserved, including various food items and textiles.

He also saw evidence of the fire. It was said that Josephus Flavius wrote that everything was burnt except the stores to leave a message to the Romans that it wasn't due to hunger that they had committed suicide. As Ken toured the Herod's palace-villa, the Throne room, the bath houses, storerooms, the western palace and the Zealots' living quarters, he was amazed at the construction and the details that still remained. Overall, though, Ken was left feeling sad that so many had died there. This was not a happy place however, it was a place where heroes had died in freedom. They did not want to die as servants to the Romans but as servants to God and they had looked on it as a gift of sorts to be able to choose to die bravely and as a free people.

The speech that Elazar ben Ya'ir had given was read by the tour guide. It was about not surrendering and the desire to be free in their own land. Ken remembered that Israel became a sovereign nation in 1948 and that the Jewish people returned to their homeland from all over the world. Masada was a special place. When he got to his hotel he read from Ezekiel 37 and he got the sense that Israel was special to God. He was struck by verse twenty-two which promised that the nation would have one king over them all.

Chapter Forty-Six
Climbing Higher

Ken could not shake the desire to explore several other places. He just knew that he had to visit these places to complete his quest for what was real and what was true. This drive propelled him forward. He would not stop until he had a sense of peace. He was now headed on a plane to Peru, in South America. As the plane roared through the clouds Ken read up on the history of Machu Picchu. It was located 2400 meters above sea level. It was a city of sorts located near a steep cliff that was 400 meters deep and which formed the canyon that leads to the Urubamba River. As Ken studied pictures of this mysterious place he felt a sense of awe at the ingenious workmanship and the back-breaking work that it had taken to construct of this place. Why all this labour? For what? As he sipped his coffee Ken read that this place had had something to do with the worship of the sun. He mused to himself that many ancient cultures had worshipped the sun, probably because in their minds it gave life to the planet. Ken could feel excitement rise in him as the flight attendant told everyone that they were beginning their descent.

    Ken decided that he'd take a train from Cusco to a town near Machu Picchu so that he could view the countryside. He went to the San Pedro station in Cusco and settled back for the 112 kilometer ride which would take him over the Picchu mountain, zigzagging all the way until the highest pinnacle called "El Arco" (the arc) was reached which was located in the northeastern part of the city. After that beginning, many sites would be seen as a descent was made gradually to the Sacred Valley of the Incas. Ken started to feel sleepy and so he slept for some of the trip. He was able to sleep for a while even though the train was jostling him around. After some stops the train came to its destination which was Aguas Calientes which was over two thousand meters high. It was getting late in the day and so

Ken headed toward a room in a lodge that he had booked. This town was only four miles away from Machu Picchu.

After a sumptuous supper in the lodge's restaurant, Ken walked around the beautiful grounds and admired the views from every aspect. He met a group of tourists who were going to go to Machu Picchu the next day. Ken was able to be included in their group. He kept craning his neck to look up at the towering mountains all around this place. He saw a group sitting together praying and he wondered why they were doing that publically. Many different types of groups came to this place and Ken guessed that they each had some particular purpose. He also saw a group dressed in various bright colors and a flash of something like subdued terror coursed through his body. It couldn't be … he wondered. He'd keep an eye out for that group. Ken was very surprised at how modern and clean his room was and that it had every comfort he required. As he looked out his window at the setting sun dipping below the towering, brooding mountains, he remembered a verse Sean had quoted that talked about the heavens declaring the glory of God and the firmament showing His handiwork. Yes, Ken believed in God but he didn't feel that he was close to Him or that he could commune with Him.

The next day dawned bright and Ken jumped out of his comfortable bed and got ready for this adventure of all adventures. He was going to see one the great wonders of the world. He had a superb breakfast and then he joined the group all lined up for the short bus ride to the ruins. Ken got a seat right at the front of the bus and next to him was a portly gentleman who was very talkative and friendly. His name was Evan and he was from New Zealand. He told Ken that this was the third time that he had visited the ruins. He informed Ken that he always saw something different every time he visited this place. He told Ken that he was glad that the Spanish had not captured Machu Picchu even though they had managed to capture and then control most of the Inca Empire. This ancient city had existed for about one hundred years. It was built around 1450 AD. Evan told Ken that Machu Picchu means Greater Summit.

Chapter Forty-Seven
A Marvel

As Ken stepped out over a rocky ledge he gasped in awe at the sight which lay below him. It was as if he was entering a time long ago and he was able to see into it in some manner. He saw the remnants of stone homes and terraces and great mountains all around. He was at Machu Picchu! The clouds seemed to be below him and he felt light-headed as he craned his head to take in all the sights. The guide gathered the group around him and told them what they would see that day. He told the eager, attentive group that the city probably had about five hundred citizens and its well-hidden location was the reason the Spanish never found it. The great mystery of this place, the guide explained, was how the great stones were moved. It clung to the side of a mountain which overlooked the Urubamba River valley. The rocks were carefully carved and fit together perfectly. The guide described the main sites. There were one hundred and forty sites to see but they would not see them all! There were temples, parks and residences which had been homes with thatched roofs and there were also sanctuaries. The guide informed them that there were more than one hundred stone steps! Water fountains and water drainage systems for irrigation had been a part of this marvelous place.

The group passed the Caretaker's Hut and the Funerary Rock and then they were on their way to the Temple of the Sun. Ken was amazed at the polished and rounded large granite blocks of its rounded walls. The guide told them that the Incas believed that Manco Capac was the first king of the Kingdom of Cusco. He was said to have been born from the sun god, Inti. Being an agricultural people, they depended upon the sun for the growth of their crops. Therefore the Temple of the Sun was dedicated to this god and it was like a solar observatory. There was a window on the ledge that sat above the temple. The sun's rays were caught at an angle from this vantage point. The constellation of Pleiades could be seen from this window. This helped the Incas to calculate when the rains would come and therefore when it was the right time to plant their crops. Ken looked at an altar which had been carved from a large boulder. It was placed in the center of this temple area where animal sacrifices were thought to have taken place. Ken remembered that the Israelites had to offer animal offerings for the forgiveness of their sins. The blood of the animals was shed for their iniquities. He wondered why he had that thought as he looked at this rock.

The next site they visited was the Intihuatana Stone. It was situated on the highest part of the area where the people lived in their homes. It was above a pyramid. The meaning of this place was a place to tie the sun or "the hitching post of the sun". It was a place to "catch" the sun on the shortest day of the year which is the winter solstice. These former inhabitants of this mysterious place knew the positions of the stars, the phases of the moon, when eclipses would occur and they fervently believed in their constellations. Rituals were performed here to appease the gods they believed controlled their destinies. The stone had a particular shape which looked something like a sun dial.

The guide let the group wander around by themselves to the other sites. Ken went to the Palace of the Princess, which was said to be connected to rituals probably at the Temple of the Sun. A female priest or virgins might have lived there as they would be involved in the rituals. The virgins might have been offered to the sun or water as sacrifices. After that Ken went to the Royal Tomb which was below the tower of the Temple of the Sun. An important person was thought to have been buried there. The rest of Ken's time was spent wandering around to get a feeling for how everything was laid out. The Sacred Plaza was a central platform which was surrounded by buildings of religious significance. Ken wondered about what rituals had been performed there and who was involved in them. Ken wandered through the Temple of the Three Windows which was located on the East side of the Sacred Plaza. It had one side open to the plaza. It was like an observation point. On the south side of the plaza was the House of the Priest and it had two doors which provided exits to the plaza. Across from the Priest's House was a temple which was considered to be the most important temple. There was a stone altar in the back wall and the side that was nearest to the plaza was open. Ken was impressed by the planning that had gone into all of these buildings.

As the daylight was starting to go, Ken and his group left the ruins. He would never forget this place and he felt he understood why this place had been constructed. That led him to think of another place he would like to visit which would hopefully help him to understand ancient peoples a little better. He wanted to tie together everything he had learned and he knew that he'd have to examine this ancient place that he would go to as soon as possible.

Chapter Forty-Eight
Mighty Stones

In no time at all it seemed that Ken was on his way to yet another adventure. He was on his way to England. He going to go to Stonehenge! This was said to also be a place arranged for a view of the skies. After making arrangements, he was able to hop on a tour bus to Wiltshire the day he arrived in England. He was looking forward to seeing this famous ancient site. The guide told the tour group some interesting facts. She said that more than nine hundred stone rings could be found in the British Isles. There may have been twice that number built. The guide stated that there had been a number of phases or periods that Stonehenge had gone through over many years. At first, Stonehenge was just a circular ditch with a bank on the inside of it. It was aligned with the midsummer sunrise and midwinter sunset and with the most southerly and also the most northerly setting of the moon. Ken remembered that Machu Picchu had similar alignments. There were fifty-six holes around the perimeter and human cremation remains had been found in them. The circle was three hundred and twenty feet in diameter and it only had one entrance. There had been a wooden sanctuary in the middle. Ken wondered what that was used for and he could only imagine what might have taken place there and then he remembered that sanctuaries and altars all seemed a part of ancient and modern worship. His mind flitted briefly to the crude circle scraped out on the mountain in Switzerland. He mumbled to himself something about things not changing and the nearby passengers gave him looks of surprise and some irritation as he was interrupting the guide's talk to them. Ken had a brief flashback run in his mind, of some of the antics he had witnessed by the groups in and around Wonder.

Ignoring Ken's comment, the guide (who was used to many different types of people) continued on in her perfectly enunciated

English accent about the next phase of the history of Stonehenge. The wooden sanctuary had been replaced with two circles of bluestones which were dolerite stones with a tint of blue. The entrance was widened and an avenue entrance (which was a widened version of the original entrance) was made with parallel ditches which were (not to Ken's surprise) aligned to the midsummer sunrise. A 'Heel Stone' was set up outside of the circle. There were eighty bluestones which had been somehow made their way from the Prescelly Mountains in Wales which were two hundred and forty miles away. Some of these stones weighed four tons! Ken thought of the building of the pyramids and the manpower that had taken to construct them.

The guide then told them about the next phase in which the bluestones had been taken down and replaced by huge Sarsen stones, which were usually eighteen feet high and weighed twenty-five tons. They came from the Avenbury stone rings which were about twenty miles to the north. Farther along in time about sixty of the bluestones were inserted in a circle inside the Sarsen circle. Nineteen other bluestones were put into a horseshoe pattern inside the circle. The guide was telling the group of avid listeners about how many hours of labour had been necessary to create these circles. Ken muttered to himself that these people were not slouches. He got a few more stares. The guide glared at him through her glasses. Ken was very tired from his plane trip and he hadn't eaten well for a long time and so he was in a state of exhaustion and he was living off a nervous energy. He wondered why he hadn't bothered to take a day or two to refresh himself and relax before dashing off to yet another of the wonders of the world. He muttered an apology to all who cared to listen to him. He thought to himself that these people were too solemn.

As the bus got near to the site Ken could hardly contain himself. There on the horizon rose the giant stones. They rose from the green earth like huge trees without leaves. They seemed to guard something on the inside. Ken knew that there were hundreds of round barrows or burial mounds (a large mound of earth or stones placed over burial sites) scattered over the Salisbury Plain on which this marvel stood. Ken felt that the modern evidences of civilization all around the site, such as: parking lots, gifts shops and ice cream stands were gaudy somehow and rather strange. Ken had become serious and he joined the group on their exploration of the site. He learned some more facts about the stones.

He learned about trilithons which were constructed of two large pillar stones which supported a third stone which sat across the tops of the stones. The trilithons were the heaviest of all the stones as they weighed about forty-five tons and they were found toward the center of Stonehenge. He saw the Slaughter Stone as they went down the Stonehenge Avenue. He also noticed that the stones increased in size as they neared the center of the monument. There was the Altar stone inside the Bluestone horseshoe stones. Ken tried to see in his mind's eye how all the stones had looked and how they had been positioned. Ken was interested to find out that the stones had differing shapes and they had alternated between being tall, to thin (like pillars) and to stones which were shaped like obelisks.

Ken didn't know what to think about what he saw that day. He had heard all the theories as to why Stonehenge had been constructed. He heard about the myths of renewal that ancient peoples practiced when the solstices and equinoxes occurred. The astronomical cycles were thought of as being special to people, animals and to the earth. It was worship of creation and then Ken stopped and realized that they had not worshipped The Creator. All over the British Isles and in Europe stone rings and barrows were constructed to be aligned with the heavens. They were trying to "trap" the sun and the moon. As Ken's tour bus drove away from Stonehenge he felt that most of his search for meaning had been achieved but there was one very, very ancient place that he had not seen and which would possibly put the "cap" on his search.

Chapter Forty-Nine
Discovery

Ken actually took some time off before he flew to his next (and he really hoped) and final destination. He visited Bath, Salisbury Cathedral and Windsor Castle - all monuments to ideals. People long ago, he told himself, again, were very smart and not shirkers. They were tougher than the so-called modern sophisticated culture. They created beauty and wonder from basic materials and many of their creations were still standing to be viewed today. As Ken sat by a window overlooking a beautiful rose garden in his hotel in Salisbury, he planned his last adventure. It would certainly not be a place as green and lush as England. He had thought of going to … Babylon (or the site of that once great city) because he knew that the Tower of Babel had probably been built there or near there because very early peoples wanted to reach heaven. How fitting would a trip to that place be as he wound up this never-ending quest that he had been on for so long. He just felt in his inner being, that he would resolve the last of his questions. He called Sean and told him about his trip and Sean thought that he'd discover something special there in the home of early civilizations.

As Ken sat in the plane that would take him to Babylon, he read some facts about this ancient place. Babylonia existed between 2700 B.C. and 500 B.C. It was an ancient area in the south of Iraq. Ken read Genesis 11 as Sean had suggested and he saw how the building of the tower of Babel could have taken place because many peoples lived there and they had plans to be great in the world's eyes. They wanted to manipulate deity and become like gods. They possibly built a ziggurat which was a terrace tower and which was common in those days. They built them to worship pagan deities. He got ready for the plane to land in Bagdad, Iraq and he was nervous and excited at the same time.

It was very fortunate that Ken was able to get a cab into Baghdad as there seemed to be few around that day. The driver told him that he could get a bus ride to Babylon with his brother who ran a tour bus line. The bus line had only one bus but Ken felt relieved that he had a way to get to his destination. Babylon was only ninety kilometers south of Baghdad. Ken enjoyed chatting with the driver as there were only a few passengers who kept to themselves at the back of the bus. The driver told Ken that tourism was really down due to the conflict currently underway and he told Ken to be ready for soldiers who might stop the bus along the way. Fortunately they weren't stopped that day. Ken could see that people had gardens behind walls around their homes. He got glimpses of green gardens and palm trees sprouted everywhere. About ten kilometers north of Hilla, the Baghdad-Hilla highway branched off to Babylon.

When the bus arrived at the site Ken was surprised. All that he saw was a mound and broken mud-brick buildings and rubble. This was Babylon? Ken was disappointed. He knew that reconstruction of Babylon was going on but he wanted to see the "real" Babylon. It was hard to imagine that there had once been hundreds of temples in this vicinity. Where were the walls and defensive towers? Babylon had been the capital of ten Mesopotamian dynasties. Most of the existing buildings belonged to the second King, who was called Nebuchadnezzar II who had reigned during the last dynasty when Babylon was at its greatest. The ruins covered thirty square kilometers. Ken was able to look at what was left of the Summer and Winter Palaces of King Nebuchadnessar II, the Ziggurat which was next to it, the Lion of Babylon, the Street of Processions and the Ishtar Gate. Ken had read that a replica had been built using some of the original materials from Babylon at the Pergamom Museum in Berlin. It was completed in the nineteen thirties.

It was hard for Ken to imagine what the real Babylon was like as he looked on the rubble before him. It was hard to believe that there had been streets running parallel and at right angles to the river and that there had been several main gates. The city had been surrounded by more than one wall. There had been security towers around the outside walls. Twenty-five years after King Nebuchadnezzar died, Babylon's greatness had passed.

Ken looked at the rebuilt section of the site. Saddam Hussein had the Southern Palace rebuilt as well as the walls of the Procession Street. Several temples have also been rebuilt. A Babylonian theater was built along with tourist facilities. There were lakes, orchards and gardens to explore - all created under Hussein's orders. What was really left of Babylon was a mound or tell which had broken mud-brick buildings and debris strewn around on the plain which was part of the Mesopotamian plain between the Tigris and the Euphrates rivers. The city had been built along the left and right banks of the Euphrates. Steep embankments had to be constructed to keep back flood waters. Yes, Ken thought to himself, the glory has departed from the grandness that had once been this city.

There was a place there where some thought the Tower of Babel had been constructed. All that Ken saw was a hole surrounded by a moat. One old man told him that there were several other places where the Tower was thought to have been built but no one was sure of the exact place. Saddam Hussein had plans to rebuild it but that had not happened. One fact that Ken learned and perhaps, it was the surprise that Sean had said he'd have there, was that after the people were scattered, the work on the tower stopped. They were dispersed everywhere around the world. They took their ideas and building plans with them. It was an idea that a lady talked to him about as they were looking at the hole that was left of what was, perhaps, the Tower of Babel. She referred him to the pyramids in Egypt and the temples around the world and the belief systems that each represented and then Ken saw that this could be true. It made sense to him that from one central place, people could take their spiritual beliefs with them and pass them down to the generations that followed them.

Chapter Fifty
Resolution

Ken flew back to Switzerland for a visit with Sean. Sean was very happy to see him and they sat down in his small living room and chatted about all that Ken had seen and done since they had parted. Ken shared his pictures with Sean and described every one of them. Several hours passed as the two friends discussed Ken's adventures. Sean said that Ken looked different somehow. Ken said that he felt that he was heading towards finally being at peace and that he had found many answers to his numerous questions. Sean wanted to know what he had learned. Ken told Sean that he had learned that God was in control of the Universe and no matter what men tried they couldn't go against what He planned or wanted to perform in the Earth and in men's lives. Sean said that Ken had made a good start. This surprised Ken as he thought that he'd learned all that he needed to know and now Sean was saying that there was more to learn! Ken mumbled something about having to go around the world looking for more clues to the mystery of life for the rest of his existence. Sean laughed loudly. Ken didn't want to talk anymore and so he changed the subject and told Sean that he wanted to settle down in one place after all of his travels but he didn't know where to go as yet. Later that day Sean told Ken that several of the "cave people" were now attending his church. Ken was puzzled but he said nothing to Sean about that 'development'.

Ken stayed with Sean for a week and then one day he announced that he was going to go to New York to open up an art gallery and maybe he'd give art lessons. Sean was surprised. Ken told him that he had always wanted to go to New York and he felt that this was one city in which he could possibly settle down and call it his home. Sean gave him the phone numbers of several people he could contact who would be good friends to him. Ken was pleased that he would have some people to get to know in that big city.

Two months later Ken was comfortably housed in an apartment overlooking Central Park and he had a flourishing art gallery several blocks down the street. Business was good and he was living a full life. He was a wealthy man without any financial worries. As he sat in a comfortable chair by his large picture window, sipping a cup of coffee one afternoon, he saw a movement in the sky. He looked closer and saw that it was an eagle soaring above the clouds very high up and he thought that was strange. He had not expected eagles to fly around an urban center. He thought that it was a sign of some kind. He decided that he would study up on the symbolism of the eagle. He remembered staring up at the eagles soaring over the mountains near Wonder. He never go tired of watching them effortlessly drifting above the Earth with freedom.

As he had time that day, he started on a search for the symbolic meaning of eagles. He soon realized that the eagle was a powerful symbol for many cultures. He wondered if this sighting of an eagle was going to help him learn some of the things he apparently needed to learn, according to Sean. Sean sent him information about eagles in the Scriptures and the verses that had eagles in them could be categorized according to several types ranging from symbolizing swiftness, to prophetic symbols, destruction and judgment, parables, renewal of youth and strength and flying toward heaven. Ken wondered what the eagle could mean for him.

One fact that Ken found out about eagles was that mother eagles had been seen with eaglets on their wings, carrying them far distances. It was a free ride. No effort on their part was required. They flew free above the earth and they were safe. Ken wished he could experience that feeling of complete rest and security without fear. Those eaglets had supreme trust in their mother. Ken had been surprised to read that mother eagles pushed eaglets out of the nest on a high mountain crag to teach them to fly. However, she did not let them fall to their deaths but rather flew beneath them and returned them to the nest. After going through this process many times, the eaglets learned to fly on their own. Sean had called him the night before and they had been talking about eagles. He referred to this very action of a mother eagle when he quoted Deuteronomy 32:11 where it says that "As an eagle stirreth up her nest, fluttereth over her young, spreadeth abroad her wings, taketh them, beareth them on her wings,". Sean had told Ken to read the next verses about how God had led Jacob to the land he was supposed to inherit and that there had been no strange god with him and that he would ride on "the high places of the earth," (verse13).

As Ken mused on what he knew now was the truth he came to the conclusion that he needed to take what some called was a leap of faith. On several occasions Sean had explained the way of redemption which God had provided through His Son, Jesus Christ. He called Sean and told him that he was ready to accept the Son of Righteousness as his own Redeemer. The Mediator would take him into His forever family. It was the family he had always wanted and he knew that after he had prayed with Sean that Sean was his brother and they would spend eternity together. It was after that call that Ken had the peace, the real peace that he had so long craved. He was God's child, a child of the Most High God. He had gone down a path that was often filled with searching people on quests for answers and far off places built by ancients who too, had searched for answers to the mysteries of life and death and what happened after one died. However, along the way he had met people who had helped him in his search. They hadn't forced their beliefs on him but rather they were kind and caused him to ask more questions. Each situation, person, group and place had been part of the puzzle that came together that sunny afternoon in New York. He knew he would never be alone again.

Chapter Fifty-One
The New Life Upon The Rock

After that great day when Ken became a child of God, he set out to live a life pleasing to Him. He was still bitten by the traveling bug at times but he didn't suddenly take off impulsively but rather worked his travels into missions of mercy for needy people around the world. His adventures continued and he was influential in pointing many to The Way, The Truth and The Life. He was never restless again because he had come to the One Who gives Rest. His further adventures in many parts of the world and in many situations are written down for all to read. Ken wrote novels and books for many years and people enjoyed reading his books because he also illustrated many pages of them. Ken was a happy man who had found wisdom and understanding. He had many favorite Bible verses. One verse held so much meaning for him and that was Psalms 97:11 which says, "Light is sown for the righteous and gladness for the upright in heart." He was always ready to assist those who had questions like he had that day so long ago when he had walked into a quaint village in the mountains. He now had been set on high places. His life was based on the Rock Christ Jesus, The Bright and Morning Star and he was enjoying the view. Some other favorite verses were: "As for God, his way is perfect; the word of the LORD is proved; he is a shield to all those who trust in him. For who is God, save the LORD? Or who is a rock, save our God? It is God who girdeth me with strength, and maketh my way perfect. He maketh my feet like hinds' feet, and setteth me upon my high places" (Psalms 18: 30-33). They were pure places and he was full of hope and peace. He didn't need to search or wonder any more. He was free like an eagle.

CPSIA information can be obtained at www.ICGtesting.com
Printed in the USA
BVOW10055211051B
333293LV00001B/12/P